The
DRUM
of DESTINY

The Drum of Destiny is published by Stone Arch Books,
A Capstone Imprint
1710 Roe Crest Drive
North Mankato, Minnesota 56003

www.mycapstone.com

Library of Congress Cataloging-in-Publication Data is
available on the Library of Congress web site.
ISBN: 978-1-4965-2673-1 (library binding)
ISBN: 978-1-4965-2674-8 (paperback)
ISBN: 978-1-4965-2676-2 (eBook)

Designer: Russell Griesmer
Cover illustration: Sam R. Kennedy
Design elements: Shutterstock

Printed and bound in the United States of America.
009745R

The DRUM of DESTINY

BY CHRIS STEVENSON

STONE ARCH BOOKS
a capstone imprint

MASSAC
NEW YORK
SPRINGFIELD
HARTFORD
CONNECTI
NEW HAVEN
MAMARONECK
NEW ROCHELLE
NEW YORK

USETTS

MARLBOROUGH   CAMBRIDGE
                        ★ ★ BOSTON
   ×
    WORCESTER
  ×

R H O D E   I S L A N D

THE POST ROAD

~ GABRIEL'S ROUTE TO BOSTON ~

Atlantic Ocean

GABRIEL

1

THE LORING HOUSE

Reverend Loring's house loomed ahead of Gabriel Cooper as he made his way along the streets of New York. While most people saw the house as large and elegant, with its two white-washed columns framing the front entrance, twelve-year-old Gabriel saw only a confined and dreary space. He could find no joy there. He did not belong.

Gabriel hadn't really belonged anywhere since his parents, a bookstore owner and his wife, died of the pox the year before. The Lorings had taken him in, but at times he wished he were living by himself on the streets.

With ten children in the Loring family, there was little food to go around, and Gabriel had barely enough food to survive. The Lorings expected him to pay for his keep, so instead of attending school, he got a job setting type at Peter Dalrymple's print shop—a job given to him because he could read and write. Many nights, he would arrive back at the house after a long day at the shop to find the table cleared, just a scrap of bread left for him. He would eat quietly and then head upstairs to find his blanket on the hard wooden floor in the corner of the Loring boys' bedroom. As he lay on the floor, he could hear the older boys snickering under their breath about the "orphan boy." Sometimes he felt like crying, but he always held back his tears, refusing to give the boys the satisfaction.

Despite the dread Gabriel felt as he neared the Loring home, the world seemed a bit brighter on that sunny spring day. He had finished early at the print shop and would make it to the Lorings in time for dinner—and a bit more food than usual. Still he knew he'd have to pay a price for being home early. Mrs. Loring would have a miserable, endless line of work for him as soon as he walked in the door. He was more of an indentured servant than a member of a family.

Gabriel endured more than just endless work and hunger in the Loring home. Reverend Loring was a strong loyalist. Every night at dinner, he condemned colonists for their lack of loyalty to the good king of England, His Majesty, King George III. Everyone around the table listened at attention and nodded in agreement—everyone, that is, except for Gabriel. This did not go unnoticed by Reverend Loring.

Gabriel longed to do more than just refuse to agree. He wished he could stand up at the Lorings' long dinner table and shout at the top of his lungs, "KING GEORGE IS A TYRANT!" But the risk was too great.

Gabriel had his reasons for siding with the patriot cause. When Gabriel's father was still alive, Gabriel heard him speak of Parliament's taxes on paper, tea, lead, and glass—and of colonists forced into taxation without representation. In other words, the colonists had to give money to the king without any say in what laws should govern them. But, more than having heard his father speak out against the unfair taxes, Gabriel knew firsthand what the king's soldiers were like.

Under the Parliament's Quartering Act, colonists had to house and feed British troops in their public businesses whenever necessary. When Gabriel was ten, two British soldiers found it "necessary" to lodge at the Coopers' bookstore. They ate the Coopers' food and drank their wine, all without paying a thing. Gabriel considered this nothing more than stealing. Even more despicable was the way the soldiers would strut around full of arrogant pride. They called the colonists worthless rabble and said they awaited the day when they could return to "glorious England, where true gentlemen lived." Gabriel's father had told him not to speak out against the soldiers, at least not in their presence, and Gabriel never did. He bottled it all in.

It was with this bottled-up resentment that Gabriel stepped back into the Loring home early that evening. He quickly shot through the door and ran upstairs before anyone noticed he was home. Rushing into the room where he slept, he pried up a loose floorboard.

Hidden under the floor were his most precious possessions: a small bit of money he had saved from his printing-press job, an old knife, a flint rock, a flask he had found by the East River, and the two most precious of all—a note that his mother had written to Gabriel not long after she had taken ill and a ring she had left him. He checked these items whenever he could to make sure that the Lorings had not touched them.

He deposited one of the two coppers he'd just earned into this secret hiding place—the other had to be given to Reverend Loring—then he waited upstairs until he heard the servants below call the family to the table.

In the dining room, Gabriel took a seat at the long wooden bench. He found a spot by Herbert, a redheaded boy about his age and the only Loring who was kind to him. There was barely any room for Gabriel at the end of the bench, but he managed to fit.

As Gabriel sat down, he was met with a cold stare from Mrs. Loring. "Gabriel, why did you not come to me directly after returning from Dalrymple's? You know the washer woman is off for the week, and there is laundry that needs tending to. I should have you leave and tend to the washing immediately, but as the grace of God wills, I will let you sit and eat first. However, the next time I find you home early from the printer's without finding work to do, you will meet with the lash. Do you understand?"

Gabriel gritted his teeth, smiled, and said, "Yes, Ma'am. Thank you, Ma'am."

With a solemn look on his face and a stern glance at Gabriel, Reverend Loring led the mealtime prayer. Once the food had been passed around the table, he began another one of his speeches on glorious England.

"A lack of respect for God-given authority is what it is—an unnatural rebellion! Have we forgotten our loyalty! Have we forgotten our rich English heritage? Not this family. We shall remain loyal to our king until the end. God, save the king, and death to bad government. And taxes? Are we not to give back to the king for the wonderful goodness he has shown these colonies? I dare say that a true English gentleman gives freely to the crown and does not complain. God forbid that we should rise up against the very king who has provided for us so richly. God save us from these traitors and rebels!"

Reverend Loring went on to tout how his grandfather had been invited to visit the king's court many times and how fortunate this made their family. He paused and looked around the table at the nodding Lorings. His eyes stopped on Gabriel. The boy's head held steady. Speaking to everyone but keeping his eyes on Gabriel, Reverend Loring said, "I am sure that Grandfather Loring—may he rest in peace—takes comfort in heaven to know that *all* people in the Loring house, young and old, are loyal to His Majesty, the king."

"Here, here," cheered John Loring, the oldest of the sons. John raised his glass, offering a toast to the glories of the king

and the Loring tradition. Everyone raised their glasses—
everyone except Gabriel.

Now all the Lorings, with their glasses still in the air,
fixed their eyes on Gabriel. "Uh-hum," the reverend uttered,
pretending to clear his throat and repeating his eldest son's
toast. "To the glories of the king and the Loring tradition."
Gabriel's glass remained as firmly situated on the table as if it
were nailed there.

Reverend Loring glared at Gabriel in disbelief. "Perhaps
you did not hear me when I said that *all* people, young and old
in the Loring house, are loyal to His Majesty, the king. Now,
young Master Cooper, raise your glass."

Gabriel's face was stern and resolute. He glared back at
Reverend Loring and spoke, "I will not drink to a *tyrant*!"

Everyone at the table gasped. Mrs. Loring slumped over
in her chair, having fainted. Reverend Loring immediately
rose and told one of his daughters to fan her mother and
another to fetch the smelling salts.

Quickly reviving his wife, the reverend now turned his
reddened face to Gabriel. "What did you call our good and
noble king? I warn you to reconsider, choosing your words
carefully," said the seething reverend.

Gabriel sat silent for a minute and carefully considered his
options. He could take back the insult he had made against
the king and the Lorings, or he could repeat the word *tyrant*.
If Gabriel recanted, he would still be punished, but he would

be allowed to stay under the Lorings' roof. If he refused to take back his words, what then? Would he really be forced to leave? Would he be sent back out on the streets? How would he survive? Where would he go?

The Lorings sat in stunned silence. Gabriel looked at each of them, and time seemed to slow. As he scanned their faces, Gabriel saw John Loring mouth the word *orphan*. No sound came from John's mouth, but Gabriel knew the word well. He would never belong here.

At that moment, something turned inside Gabriel. Like the ships he had seen in the river that drop sail and change course with the wind filling their sails, Gabriel would take a new course—a course away from this house.

Gabriel spoke without hesitation, "I called the king of England a tyrant." He went on, "He is a mean, oppressive, and brutal ruler who thinks he is above the law and can do whatever he wishes. He is not worthy of obedience and certainly not worthy of a toast with my glass."

With that, Mrs. Loring fainted again, this time falling all the way to the floor. While two daughters rushed to revive her, Reverend Loring pointed at the door and shouted, "Master Gabriel Cooper, pack up your belongings and leave this home! You have shamed this family before the eyes of God and our king. I will not tolerate such heathen and disrespectful behavior! You, child, have been spoiled by traitors, and I will not have you near my family!"

The entire Loring family stared in wide-eyed amazement, their cups having now been placed firmly back on the table. Gabriel left the room. Trying not to look back at the piercing stares, he climbed the stairs up to the bedroom corner.

Gabriel pried up the floorboard and began to gather his only possessions. He spread out the single blanket the Lorings had given him and laid out his treasures in the middle. When he picked up his mother's ring and note, he paused for a moment, holding the prized items in his hand.

The ring was too big for Gabriel to wear, so he kept it in his pocket most of the time. The gold band held a beautiful blue jewel, along with a strange yellow symbol that looked like open flower petals. A few random letters and markings were carved on the side of the ring, but they made no sense to Gabriel. His mother had once told him the ring was a French family heirloom and the blue jewel was a sapphire. The ring was precious to Gabriel, not because of what it might be worth, but because it reminded him of his mother.

The note brought back memories of his mother, as well. Gabriel had read that note many times since his mother had died. He did not understand much of it, but one thing was clear: his mother had loved him very much.

Gabriel put the ring in his pocket and finished wrapping his other things in a small blanket. He was tying up the bundle when Herbert Loring came into the room. "I got you some dried meat and biscuits from mother's kitchen for you to take along," he said. "I am sorry Father says you have to leave us. He might let you stay if you come back down and apologize."

Gabriel looked up at the fair-skinned boy who stood before him. "Thank you, but I will not apologize for telling the truth. I knew this day would come. I just did not think it would be quite this soon."

"Where will you go? What will you do?" asked Herbert.

Those were hard questions to which Gabriel had no answer. "I don't know, Herbert, but it does not matter right now. All that matters is that I am leaving this house, and I am not returning."

Herbert looked at him in amazement. Gabriel knew that Herbert had come to look up to him. Herbert had asked Gabriel to teach him French, just as Gabriel's mother had taught him. He had told Gabriel that he wanted to read all of the same books that Gabriel had been able to read in his father's bookstore. Gabriel knew that Herbert admired his determination and sense of adventure. Still, he was surprised when Herbert blurted out, "I would like to come with you, wherever you are going."

Gabriel shook his head. "No, you wouldn't. Your place is here, Herbert. You are a Loring. You have a future in this home. I do not." He was surprised that Herbert was willing to throw away the one thing that Gabriel wanted more than anything: a family.

Herbert did not press him any further. "If I cannot go, then I will pray for you, Gabriel. Every night, under my breath, of course. I would pray out loud, but I am afraid that if Father knew I was praying for a, tra . . . You know, a trait—"

"Just say it, Herbert. A *traitor*. You think I am a traitor to the crown."

"No," answered Herbert. "I do not think you are a traitor, but Father does. I will pray out loud, Gabriel, if you think that God will listen more closely."

Gabriel, with his sack full of belongings in hand, put his hand on Herbert's shoulder. "Herbert, God listens to us, no matter what. At least that is what my mother and father told me. Say your prayers in silence and save yourself from your father's lash. Now, I have to go."

With that, Gabriel headed down the stairs. Thankfully, the Lorings had left the table. He opened the door and stepped into the fading daylight. Looking back, he could see Herbert's face through the small pane window from the bedroom. Herbert raised a hand and pressed it to the window. Gabriel raised his hand slowly, then put it down, and turned away. He felt alone. Although his chest began to heave, he did not cry. Gabriel knew he had a new path to find.

2

RIVER'S EDGE

With no idea where he would go or what he would do, Gabriel decided to walk to the one place he'd found some peace in the days after his parents' deaths. He had spent hours sitting on the edge of the East River, watching the ships come into the docks to have their cargos of tea, glass, furniture, spices, cloth, and all other types of English finery unloaded and then reloaded with cargos of grain, tobacco, and furs. The bustle of the work and the beauty of the ships helped take his mind away from his pain. Before the Lorings had taken him in, he even thought of stowing away on one of the ships anchored in the harbor.

Perhaps now he could sail off and leave his anguish behind. But he knew what could happen to stowaways if they were discovered. They faced a life of hard labor to work off payment for passage, or worse still, a toss over the side rail into the ocean.

He walked toward Queen Street to head south to the docks. With the sun beginning to set, the two- and three-story buildings cast their shadows on the streets. He'd just rounded the corner onto Queen Street when a swarthy-looking boy about his age sidled up alongside him. "You wouldn't happen to have a copper to spare for a poor boy like myself, would you?"

Gabriel looked at the boy, his clothes tattered and dirty. In contrast, Gabriel's clean and tidy appearance must have made the boy think he had some wealth. "I don't have any coppers to spare," replied Gabriel. As he spoke, he saw another silent, smaller boy slinking along in the shadows.

"What about a piece of bread or cheese?" continued the swarthy boy. "I am a Christian boy, you know. Go to church every Sunday. No ill living for me. Clean as a mountain stream, am I."

Out of the corner of his eye, Gabriel saw the small boy dart from the shadows. Quickly Gabriel tucked his sack full of belongings under his arm and kicked out at the small boy as he flew past him. The kick was enough to send the boy sprawling to the ground. The older boy began to reach for Gabriel's sack, but before his grubby hands could grab it, Gabriel screamed out as loud as he could, "Pickpockets!"

A woman across the street noticed what was going on and began to scream. The pickpocket boys knew that once the alarm was sounded, their work for the night was over. Soon a constable would appear, and if someone got a good look at their faces, their work as pickpockets might be over for good. They ran down an alley and back into the shadows.

Orphans were drawn to these gangs of pickpockets like flies to honey, not only to earn a living by lifting purses, but also to belong to a family again. As Gabriel watched the boys dash back into the shadows, he saw himself. Was this his destiny—to become a scrawny pickpocket? What would his mother and father say? They would be ashamed, of course, but they couldn't have known how much he longed to have a family again, even if it was with a gang of thieves.

He looked out at the East River as it came into view and tried to clear his thoughts of pickpockets. The sky began to turn orange with the setting sun, and the river began to glow as if it was on fire. He went to the stony beach where he had found some of his treasures over the past month. The knife and flint rock had floated to shore in a small wooden box, and the flask had just enough air trapped in it for him to find it bobbing a few feet out in the water.

Gabriel sat on a piece of driftwood on the stone-covered beach and looked out over the rippling water. A few lanterns glowed on the boats anchored out in the river. The lights bobbed gently up and down with the gentle waves rolling across the water. As he sat watching the lights, something along the shore caught his eye. The fading sunlight reflected off something in the water. It bobbed up and down, floating toward the shore.

Gabriel stood and took a few steps to the very edge of the water. The river lapped up against the soles of his leather shoes as he peered out over the water. Unsure what this strange object floating in on the tide might be, he took off his shoes and socks, rolled up his pants, and waded out into the river. The rocks at the bottom hurt Gabriel's feet, but his mind was focused on grabbing whatever bobbed in front of him. He reached down into the water and pulled upward to reveal a drum with a tangled strap dangling down into the water. The instrument was waterlogged and caked in mud, but he thought it could be salvaged. He was used to salvaging things that others tossed aside.

He leaned down, stuck the drum back in the water, and rubbed his hands over it, loosening the mud caked along the sides and bottom. Picking it back up out of the water, he looked at it proudly. It had a certain shine to it now as he held it up to the glowing sky.

Gabriel walked back over to the log and set the drum down in front of him. The drumskin still seemed tight. He tapped it lightly, and it gave a soggy ring. A drum . . . what could he do with a drum? He could try to sell it, but he wasn't sure what kind of price it would bring. The demand for drums in New York wasn't high, not like in Boston, where some ten thousand troops had gathered to drive the hated redcoats from town. The British had sailed their ships into Boston Harbor and taken over the town, driving out any citizens who were not loyal to the crown. Selling the drum in New York might not even buy a single day's worth of food, but in Boston, some drummer boy would undoubtedly pay well to have his own drum.

Still, even in New York, he'd seen soldiers marching to the cadence of a drum played by a boy about his age. He loved the rolling sound of the drums and how that sound led the soldiers' every step, perfectly timed to the rhythm. If only he knew how to play the drum, he could be a drummer boy.

A vision came to him. It felt as if a candle had been lit in a dark and lonely space. All the shadows were gone, and a path had opened. He would not sell this drum in New York or even in Boston. This was *his* drum, and he would learn to play it.

When his parents were alive, he often read books to learn how to do new and interesting things. Maybe he could find a book to teach him how to play the drum. Maybe someone else could teach him. Surely there were other drummer boys around Boston who could help him learn.

Boston was far away, and Gabriel had no horse and very little money. Still, he and his drum belonged there. He felt it. The excitement of this decision was nearly overwhelming. Why couldn't he journey to Boston to join a militia and fight against the tyrant king? He had good walking legs that carried him all over New York. He wouldn't have to stow away on a boat or join a family of thieving pickpockets. Nobler work awaited him.

By now, the sun was throwing its last rays of light on the world. It would be dark soon, and he didn't want to stay a minute longer in the city. His mind was set, and he wouldn't let anything or anyone turn him away. With the drum over his shoulder and his meager belongings tied up in a small blanket, he turned away from the East River and began walking.

Gabriel had never been outside New York. He knew that Boston was some two hundred miles north along the Post Road, but other than that, he wasn't sure how he was going to get to there. Boarding a ship to Boston wouldn't be possible. He'd read in newspapers that the Royal Navy was more vigilant than ever in Boston's harbor, since the destruction of the tea on Griffin's Wharf over a year ago. No merchant ships were allowed to leave or enter the port without special approval by the king. He would have to travel by land to Boston and cross King's Bridge at the very northern tip of the island of Manhattan.

Gabriel wound his way through the city streets, heading north. He stopped when he came to Cherry Street. Pausing, he couldn't help but look down the street where his old home stood. He was ready to leave New York, but not before saying goodbye to the last place where he was loved. His father's old bookstore was only a few buildings down. It was a simple store with room for the Coopers to live above the shop.

After the Lorings took in Gabriel, he sometimes wandered out and stood in front of the building, remembering the happy life he had known there. His father, James, had worked hard as a clerk to a London bookseller before sailing to the colonies with his new bride, Anne-Laurel, in tow. In a matter of months, he was able to open up this bookstore in New York. He was so proud of his shop.

Not long after the Coopers' arrival in New York, Gabriel was born. Blessed with this one and only child, the following years were good for the Coopers, and James was able to stock his shop with books from France and England. Gabriel learned to read at a young age and spent as much time as he could in his father's bookstore. Like his father, he loved books. His mother taught him to read and write French, as well. Although he went to school, he learned most of what he knew from his parents and from reading books.

Those afternoons in his father's bookstore seemed like a distant memory now as he stood in front of the dark windows. When his father and mother died, creditors came and took James Cooper's books as payment for debts he owed. The bookstore and room above it were taken, too. After that, it lay empty and dark.

Now, in the empty street, Gabriel said goodbye to the bookstore and his parents one last time. "Father and Mother, I hope you understand that I cannot stay here and keep an eye on the empty shop anymore. I found a drum in the river today, and I know it may sound strange, but I'm going to go to Boston to be a drummer in a militia. I don't know how to play yet, but I'll learn. You always taught me to decide on a path and not stray from it. Well, this is the path I'm choosing. I hope you understand, and I hope to make you proud. I love you always."

With that, Gabriel turned away. He could no longer hold back his tears. Misty-eyed, he could barely see where he was going as he crossed the Broad Way to reach Lispenard's Meadows. The air was clear and warm for an April night, and the frogs and crickets began their nighttime serenade. He found a large oak tree in the middle of a meadow not far from the dirt road he was on and decided it was as good a place as any to rest for the night. He spread out his blanket and lay down, gazing up at the stars.

A gentle breeze rustled the branches overhead, and as he looked up at the night sky, he wondered how many nights he would have to spend sleeping under the stars before he reached Boston. He figured he could walk twenty miles a day, which meant it would take him at least a couple of weeks to get there. He had shillings to buy food along the way, but he certainly did not have enough to pay for a room every night of his journey. Yes, sleeping under the stars was something he'd have to get used to. As these thoughts drifted through his head, he dozed off and did not wake until the morning light shone upon his face.

★3★
BEN'S ADVICE

In the morning, Gabriel took a bite of the dried meat and biscuit that Herbert had given him the night before, drank a sip of water from a nearby stream, and rolled up his meager belongings into his blanket. He slung the pack and his drum over his back and set off on the road toward King's Bridge. To leave the island, he would need to pass the village of Harlem, then onto King's Bridge. He'd heard of men traveling to and from King's Bridge in a day, so he figured he'd reach the bridge by noon.

After his second rest of the day, however, he realized that his twenty miles a day might be overly optimistic. Fearing that Reverend Loring would try to find him and force him to return, he left the road whenever he heard approaching hoof beats. He thought it best to avoid other travelers until he got over King's Bridge. But constantly darting off the road made for a slow journey's start. Before he knew it, the sun was already on its downward path, and he had just passed Harlem.

Finally, Gabriel saw a few buildings ahead, scattered around a bridge that crossed the Harlem River. The road had become increasingly rugged and uphill, and by the time he had reached the scattered buildings, he was so worn out that he didn't care who saw him. As he walked down the road, he saw that one of the buildings had a sign hanging out front: "King's Bridge Tavern."

Gabriel was hungry and tired. He slowly opened the door to the tavern to see what he could find. He stepped through the door and saw a bar and several tables scattered around the room. Behind the bar was a dark-haired man with a billowed shirt and white linen smock. Men dressed in simple hunting shirts and trousers sat around many of the tables. Others were dressed up, with waistcoats, breeches, and wigs.

A hard-looking man in a faded red jacket sat at the end opposite the door. A bayoneted musket leaned against his table. At first, Gabriel thought he might be one of the king's soldiers, but as he looked more closely at his clothing, it became clear he was not wearing a real uniform. One other smaller man sat at the same table. He had dark, pudgy rings under his eyes and was dressed in a shabby, brown ditto suit. He eyed Gabriel with his dark eyes as he sipped from his cup of ale. Then he gave a nudge to the muscular man in the faded red jacket and whispered something in his ear. The two strangers stared at Gabriel and his drum.

Gabriel quickly ducked in along the wall by the barkeep, trying to avoid the prying eyes of these strange men. He covered his drum with his outer coat, sat down at the bar, and tried to look relaxed, despite the quickening pace of his heart. Who were these men who seemed so interested in him and his drum? He pulled out his coin pouch from the rolled-up blanket and reached up to the black-haired barkeep.

"Could I get some meat and bread, please, sir?"

"You got coppers, laddie?" asked the gruff man.

"Yes, sir. I have some coins," said Gabriel.

"That'll be six coppers if you want a mug of cider with it."

Six coppers! Gabriel worked for a whole week for that much. If this was what meals cost, he'd be out of coppers well before reaching Boston.

Gabriel began to reach into his coin pouch to pull out the coppers, when someone's hand grabbed his shoulder. He turned, half expecting to see the hard man in the red jacket standing beside him.

Instead, he saw a tall man dressed in country clothes leaned up against the bar. "Six coppers for a slice of meat and bread, Henry? Your prices must have gone up in a hurry. As I recall, I've been coming in here and ordering meat, bread, and a mug of cider for close to five years, and last time I ordered such a meal, it cost me two coppers. Come to think of it, that's what I'm eating and drinking now, and I'll be a horned toad if that meat, bread, and mug of cider didn't cost me two coppers. Now, unless you're planning to give this young man a bottle of your finest Madeira wine with his dinner, I think you best charge this here patriotic lad a fair price. Don't cha' know he's clearly headed north to join our troops in the cause of liberty and justice."

Speechless, Gabriel looked up at this man. Did he know Gabriel somehow?

The man behind the bar glared at the farmer. "And what if I have a different charge for you than I have for strangers traveling through this here tavern?"

"Well then," said the farmer. "I will just have to let your loyalist guest Bradford Grimm know what you think about the king's taxes on your tavern and how much you hated having to house the king's soldiers without getting any pay for their food and lodging. He's sitting right over there in the faded red jacket. I'm sure he would enjoy finding another patriot traitor to crucify."

"Now, Ben, don't ya go doing that. You know what Grimm does to those he don't think is loyal to the king. We all know he and his gang of loyalist lackeys burnt down Old Man Newton's tavern. They're worse than the lobsterbacks, if you ask me. He and that rat Hannigan sit at that table, just waiting for a reason to pounce on some poor patriot. I don't like it one bit, but I can't do a thing about it. Now, I was just having a bit o' fun with the lad here. I was going to charge him two coppers for his meal all along. Sit down o'er there," said the man, "and I'll bring it out to ya, boy."

Gabriel handed over some coins out of his pouch. The man behind the counter gave him some change, and he stuck it in his pocket. Carefully picking up his covered drum and satchel, he walked to a table across the room, Grimm's eyes following him the whole way. He thought about running out the door right then and there, but that would only draw more attention.

Instead, he tried to pretend like he didn't notice Grimm watching his every move. He put his coin pouch back into his rolled-up blanket and set his drum down on the floor beside him. He took a seat, thinking the farmer who helped him would come introduce himself, but the farmer continued to lean against the bar, not even glancing his way.

After a short while, the barkeep brought out a slice of meat, bread, and a mug of cider. Gabriel dug in. He was famished from all the walking he had done that day. Although the meat was a bit dry and the bread was less than fresh, he didn't care. He needed the nourishment.

When he was nearly finished, the table of farmers got up to head out the door, but the one who had helped him didn't leave. He shook hands with his friends at the door, then walked over to Gabriel's table and pulled up a chair.

The farmer just sat without saying a word. Finally, Gabriel broke the awkward silence. "How do you know that I am headed north to join the militia at Boston? Do you know me from somewhere?"

"I know where you're headed and what you're up to because I'm not blind," said the farmer. "My name is Ben

Daniels. I farm not far from here. As far as me knowing where you're headed, you have a drum with you, do you not?"

"Yes," replied Gabriel.

"You got mud on your shoes, having walked north all day from New York, have you not? Getting ready to cross the bridge, aren't you?"

"Yes," replied Gabriel again.

"And north of here lies Massachusetts, where there has been fighting at Lexington and Concord, and where a militia has been gathering to drive the redcoats out of Boston?"

"Yes . . . yes," said Gabriel.

"And boys your age have dreams about leading troops into a glorious battle victory, beating your drum as the soldiers march along to the beat?"

"Yes, that's all true, but I still don't know how you figured all that out from just looking at me," said Gabriel.

"I told you I'm not blind," chuckled Ben. "The one thing I *don't* know is where your ma and pa are and why they're letting such a young lad take off to fight the enemy."

Gabriel swallowed hard. "My mother and father both died of smallpox last year. They only lived a month after getting sick, dying within a week of each other. I got a touch of the pox but never took ill the way they did."

"I feared as much," Ben responded with a solemn nod. "The good Lord says for us to help widows and orphans, so I have a few things to say to you. Listen up." Ben pulled his chair up closer to the table. "Now, you have a long way to go to get to Boston, and you have a lot to learn about being wise to your surroundings. I would let you have a horse of mine if I had one to spare, but I'm afraid I don't. But I *will* give you what I *do* have, and that is my advice, as long as you're willing to sit here and listen to an old farmer."

"I will gladly listen, sir," said Gabriel.

"First things first, what is your name?" asked Ben.

"Gabriel Cooper."

"Well, Master Cooper, do you know all about what happened at Lexington and Concord only just a few weeks ago?"

Not wanting to appear unknowing, Gabriel stuttered, "Of . . . of course." In truth, he knew very little about what had happened. The newspapers in New York had stories about shots being fired, leading to a skirmish. Patriot papers wrote of blood having been spilled in the name of liberty. Tory papers downplayed the events, exclaiming the success, bravery, and honor of the king's troops.

Ben looked at him intently. "I said I would give you advice, and here is the first piece. When someone is willing to tell you something that you do not know much about, listen. Even if you are the smartest person in the world, you pretend to be dumb as a rock and listen. You are bound to learn something. Got it?"

"Yes, sir," replied Gabriel.

"Now we will try this again. Do you know all about what happened at Lexington and Concord?" asked Ben.

"No, sir," said Gabriel.

"Much better, my boy," replied Ben as he slapped the table. "Mind you now, all that I'm about to tell you comes straight from my brother Jacob's mouth. He's a blacksmith and a militiaman who has a house in the town of Lexington. It all started late at night when my brother was out taking care of a newborn calf. He heard someone on horseback shouting, 'The regulars are coming out!' Turns out it was a man by the name of Revere who spread the word through the Massachusetts countryside. All those militiamen knew to grab their muskets and protect their homes. Old General Gage thought he would be able to walk right in and capture Sam Adams, Hancock, and all the other Sons of Liberty without a fight. Well, he was wrong, by golly. The lobsterbacks got a fight, all right, and decided they best leave Misters Adams and Hancock alone and head on to Concord, where the patriots had a supply of weapons and ammunition. Do you understand?" asked Ben.

Gabriel thought for a second. He had heard of Sam Adams and John Hancock and knew the Sons of Liberty spoke for the rights of patriots. He had read in a newspaper that the king was furious and had declared Massachusetts in open rebellion. The king had charged Adams and Hancock with high treason and called for their arrest. But Gabriel had never heard of Revere. "Who is Mr. Revere, and how did he know the regulars were marching out of Boston?"

"Mr. Revere—Paul's his first name—lived in Boston. He figured that one day the soldiers were bound to leave Boston Neck to capture Sam Adams and John Hancock, up in Lexington. He also heard that the redcoats were going to capture the militia's supply of guns and ammunition. So Revere, along with a few others, formed a plan to alert the militia throughout the Massachusetts countryside as to when the regulars were on the march."

"How did they get out of Boston without the regulars knowing?" By now Gabriel was mesmerized by Ben's telling of the events.

"Well, now," responded Ben, "getting out of Boston was no small feat. One man rode out at night just before the sentries sealed off the neck. Revere, himself, rowed ashore to Charlestown, right between two of His Majesty's ships. Had the redcoats in those ships seen Revere sneaking across the river that time of night . . . well, he might not have made his ride."

"I'm glad he was able to sneak past the ships and get out of Boston," Gabriel responded.

"As am I," said Ben. "They won the race out of Boston against the British. General Gage's columns did not leave until a couple of hours after these brave riders had warned the militiamen. About seven hundred regulars marched all night. They reached Lexington Green at about the time the sun was coming up. When they got to the town, right there in front of them at the far edge of the green, stood the militiamen, including my brother, Jacob, guns in hand and standing proud. We should all be proud of these men, Gabriel. My brother and seventy-six men on the Green up against seven hundred of His Majesty's finest. Those patriots stood their ground. What a sight that would have been," said Ben, gazing off in a trance.

Through Ben's words, Gabriel could feel the tension and excitement those militiamen must have experienced. To think, he had not even crossed the King's Bridge yet, and he was already in the presence of the brother of a patriot who had fought the redcoats. "What happened next?" he asked, anxiously waiting to hear more.

"Right, right," said Ben. "What happened next? Well, the redcoats did not turn away, and neither did the militia. A shot was fired. My brother did not know which side fired it, but after those men heard it, they all started blasting away. The Lexington militia couldn't hold their ground against so many soldiers, so they had to give way. But that doesn't mean they gave up the fight. Many of those men, including my brother, followed the king's soldiers all along their march to Concord. After the regulars met heavy fire from the militia in Concord, they turned around to head back to Boston. By then, the men in surrounding towns heard about what was happening and gathered to make the lobsterbacks sorry for firing lead at their friends and neighbors. They chased them back to Boston. Many a redcoat dropped to the ground. It was a bloody day, Gabriel . . ." Ben's voice trailed off to silence.

Gabriel sat quietly, waiting for Ben to speak.

"Well, now, Master Cooper, let me tell you this: War is full of blood and misery. But, you know, there are some things worth fighting for, and freedom is one of them. If we had let those troops march through the Massachusetts countryside, capture Sam and John, and then destroy barns and homes that are rightfully ours, we would be living in fear. And living in fear is . . . well, it's no way to live. We paid the price in blood to make those lobsterbacks think twice about parading about the countryside."

Gabriel knew what Ben was saying. He remembered what it felt like when the soldiers stayed in their bookstore, all by order of the king. A few years ago, he also witnessed a group of the king's soldiers barge into William Darby's print shop near the Coopers' bookstore and tear apart Mr. Darby's printing press all because he was suspected of distributing papers denouncing the king and calling him a tyrant. He watched poor Mr. Darby plead with the lieutenant, asking him to identify who falsely accused him. The officer only drew his sword and threatened to run him through. Gabriel's father tried to help Mr. Darby repair the presses, but they were a total loss. Mr. Darby's livelihood was ruined. He left New York to work on his brother's farm in West Jersey. Gabriel's mother cried when Mr. Darby loaded his cart of his belongings and said his goodbyes to his friends. Gabriel never forgot how angry he was about the way good Mr. Darby was treated that day by that officer.

"Gabriel, mark my words: as long as there are redcoats over here, armed and ready for battle, there will be fear and oppression," stated Ben. "That is why all the militias are gathered around Boston right now, trying to hold those redcoats to the city. Those militiamen will not leave until the redcoats do."

"Then I know that is where I belong," said Gabriel.

Ben looked quietly at Gabriel, his eyes fixed on him. "I don't know you well, Gabriel Cooper, but I would guess there is more to your story than just a boy running away because he wants to see how a battle looks. You seem to have some wisdom beyond your young years. I am not sure where that comes from in such a young lad, but don't lose it."

"It comes from my parents," answered Gabriel. "They taught me."

"If you don't mind, tell me a little more about your ma and pa."

Gabriel smiled. "My mother, Anne, was born in France. When she was nineteen, her family visited London, and that's where she met my father, James. As you probably can guess, my mother didn't return to France with her parents. She and my father fell in love and were married. They saved their money and left England to start a new life in New York."

"And do you speak French?" asked Ben.

"*Oui, monsieur. Je parle Français.* My mother taught me," answered Gabriel.

Ben chuckled. "Well then, I am impressed. Use whatever skills it takes for you to reach Boston." Ben leaned across the table and patted him on the hand.

In that moment, Gabriel thought of how his father used to reach across the dinner table and pat him on the hand while talking to him. A small tear came to his eye. He quickly grabbed his hand away from Ben and wiped the tear that he could now feel tracing down his cheek.

"Well," stuttered Gabriel abruptly, "I had better get going. I have a long way to go, and I want to cross King's Bridge before it gets too late."

Just as he began to stand, the tavern door flew open. Two men stood on either side of a teenage boy a few years older than him. The boy had a large cut across his forehead, and his right eye was filled in with swollen purpled flesh. They dragged the battered boy between them, knocking over several chairs and a table as they brought him before the chiseled face of Bradford Grimm. The entire tavern fell silent as Grimm stood from his table. "What do we have here?"

The two lanky young men holding the boy by the arms stood proudly. The one on the left held his pointed nose in the air and spoke in a nasally tone. "We found him handing out treasonous pamphlets on the north side of the city. He claims he was just doing it to earn a few coppers and that he cannot read. He claims not to know what the pamphlets say."

With that, the boy spluttered out his plea, "It's true, sir. I swear it's true. I ain't had no teaching on readin' and writin'. Oh, please, sir, I ain't got no ma or pa. I just was looking to earn a little coin, that's all. That's all, I swear, I swear."

Grimm slapped the boy across the face. Blood spattered on the table, and the boy began to whimper in pain. "Enough!" shouted Grimm with an air of pompous authority. "I do not believe for a second that you had no knowledge of what you were doing. Give me one of your pamphlets."

Gabriel was furious. He wasn't sure what he was going to do to Grimm, but he had to do something. These loyalists were beating an innocent boy, who was obviously nothing more than an ignorant street urchin. Gabriel began to stand, but Ben quickly pulled him back down and subtly shook his head, mouthing the word, "No."

The squat, toad-like man with the dark, pudgy eyes ripped off the boy's coat and reached into his pocket. He pulled out a handful of papers and gave one to Grimm. Grimm scanned over the paper and then looked around the tavern, transfixing his eyes on every occupant as if he were a stage actor about to deliver the most important lines of a performance. "I read to you now the words of Alexander Hamilton, a known traitor to the crown: 'No man has any moral power to deprive another of his life, limbs, property or liberty; nor the least authority to command, or exact obedience from him; Our King and his Parliament are subversive of our natural liberty,'" he read with growing anger, "'because an authority is assumed over us, which we by no means assent to! For such authority can never exist while we have no part in the making of the laws that are to bind us!'"

Grimm slammed the pamphlet down on the table. "Treason against the king! Treason, I say!" He continued his gaze around the tavern. "Who among you supports this unnatural rebellion—this rejection of God's will? Who believes that we are to live without the king's authority over us? Who is willing to stand for this unholy division that leads us down the road to anarchy, to disorder, to chaos, to treason?"

Gabriel was about to boldly step from the table and confront Grimm. It was no different than standing up against Reverend Loring. Ben's eyes went wide, and he whispered, "Do not move a muscle. He will kill you."

Ben's words froze Gabriel. Kill him? Would this man really kill him?

Gabriel stood motionless as Bradford Grimm continued. "This is the New York that I know. You are the people who are loyal to the king. We are the ones who must help to crush this rebellion."

Grimm lowered his head, as if his performance was complete. Then he grabbed the boy standing weakly in front of him. With his massive hand, he took the boy's chin and forced his wobbly head up. "Tell me, boy, who is printing these pamphlets containing the words of a known traitor?"

The boy cowered, clearly expecting another blow. "I don't know . . . I don't know," he sobbed.

Grimm leaned over and yanked the bayonet from his musket. He took its gleaming point and held it next to the boy's throat. "I will ask this one more time. Who is printing these pamphlets?"

Gabriel could no longer hold himself back. He pushed his chair back and grabbed it firmly in his hands. He was about to fling it at Grimm, when, suddenly, the boy croaked out an answer. "Cavendish. The man where I got the pamphlets . . . his name is Cavendish. He has a store in the city. That's all I know, I swear."

Grimm let the bayonet fall away from the boy's throat. As he did, Gabriel released his grip on the chair. Grimm reattached his bayonet and then raised his musket in the air. "You will take us to this Cavendish. Who will go with me to weed out this rebel?"

Grimm's men whooped around him. A few other men in the tavern joined the mob and stormed out of the tavern. Gabriel sat at the table, his heart still racing. Ben must have sensed Gabriel's shock and anger. He spoke in a soothing voice. "I know you wanted to help, but it would not have done any good. Bradford Grimm is a twisted man. There was nothing we could have done to help that boy."

Gabriel swallowed hard. "Will they let him live?"

Ben nodded. "I suspect they will, for now. But I would be lying if I didn't tell you that traitors are hanged."

Gabriel didn't know what to say, so he said nothing. He just sat in silence, trying to comprehend all that had happened.

Ben went up to the tavern keeper, said something to the man, and passed him what looked to be some coins. He returned to the table and told Gabriel, "There is a room upstairs for you here tonight. You need a good night's rest before you set out from Manhattan Island."

"But—"

"But nothing, son. You listen to me. Your journey will be long and full of peril. What you saw here tonight is just a taste of the turmoil that is about to begin. You are among friends here. You need your rest. Now, you get on upstairs."

"Thank you, sir," replied Gabriel in disbelief.

"No need to thank me. A couple more important things, though, before I leave," said Ben. "First, there are likely to be loyalists just like Bradford Grimm along the Post Road between King's Bridge and Boston. When you hear hoofbeats approaching, you best get off the side of the road and into the grass or bushes. If they find a young lad toting a drum, they're not likely to believe you're just out for a Sunday stroll. They'll know where you're headed and with whom you're aiming to join."

"I had been doing this when I first started out, since I was still so close to New York. I will continue to do so, if you think it a good idea."

"That I do. Second, I know your ma and pa and the good Lord tell you not to lie, but there are times when a lie can serve a higher and nobler cause. There's nothing wrong with telling a lie to save your hide, lad, so that you might reach Boston and serve this fight for freedom well. Does that make sense to you, son?"

Gabriel had never really given any thought to having to lie. His parents had always been honest people. He had heard the Reverend Loring teach that lying lips were an abomination to the Lord. But the Bible also said not to murder one another, and certainly men had to die at the hand of another man in battle. With these thoughts swimming in his mind, he muttered, "I guess it makes sense."

"Well, I don't expect you to understand things that philosophers and theologians have struggled to understand for centuries. Now, there is one more important thing I need to tell you before I leave. There's someone you need to find when you reach the militia camps around Boston. Ask for a man named Nathaniel Greene. He's a cousin of mine from Rhode Island, and he's as cunning as a wild turkey, strong as an ox, and courageous as a lion. My brother writes that Nathaniel has his own band of militia—Rhode Islanders—and is headed up to help with things in Boston. You find him and tell him that Ben Daniels sent you to him. Knowing Nathaniel, he's liable to want some kind of proof that you know me. You tell him that you know he didn't catch that thirty-pound codfish out in the bay with his line and bait. Crazy thing jumped in our rowboat. We told everyone in town that he caught it. We were just boys and didn't think any harm would come of it, but it's something I'm sure he's never forgotten."

"I will find him, and I will tell him," said Gabriel, a smile beginning to break out across his face.

"That a boy. The codfish story is sure to catch his attention. Now, I better get going, young Master Cooper. The missus is probably wondering if I got lost." Ben stood up, put a hand on Gabriel's shoulder, and patted him on the back. "You'll be a fine soldier, Gabriel Cooper, but I don't think you'll have much use for that drum of yours."

Gabriel gave Ben a puzzled look and said, "I'm not sure what you mean, but I do thank you for everything you've done for me."

"I don't believe there are many things in this life that happen just by chance," replied Ben. "And our meeting tonight surely was not one of them." Then he turned and headed out the door into the night.

Keeping his drum concealed under his coat, Gabriel headed up to his room for the night. As he lay alone in his bed, he thought about Bradford Grimm. Feelings of anger and fear swam in his head. He was angry that loyalists like Grimm could inflict so much pain and loss and then turn around and claim they were carrying out God's will for the glory of the king. He felt sick to his stomach just thinking about it.

Despite his rage, he was scared. Opposing loyalists—and the king's soldiers, for that matter—could mean death. He had never really thought about the danger he placed himself in just by carrying a drum to Boston, but he could see the danger now.

He thought for a brief moment about going back. It wasn't too late. He could drop the drum anywhere and head back. But head back to what? There was nothing for him in New York—nothing but painful memories and the detestable Lorings.

He had no choice but to continue, and with his drum in tow. Despite what Ben said about him not needing it, Gabriel believed it was central to his plan. Without his drum, he had no hope of ever finding a militia that would want to take him on as a recruit. He was too young and too inexperienced.

He blew out his candle and tried to empty his head of the hundreds of thoughts bouncing around inside. Finally sleep came.

★ 4 ★

THE JOURNEY BEGINS

Gabriel awoke after a good night's rest and walked over to the window looking out over the road. The King's Bridge lay below. No king's soldiers appeared at the bridge, but as he watched, a small group of armed men crossed, heading north on horseback. Gabriel had no way of knowing if they were patriots or loyalists. As the sun began to rise, he knew he would have to take his chance.

He headed down the stairs with his drum in hand. Instead of the bearded man from the night before, a woman in a brown dress stood behind the bar with a broom. She stopped sweeping and watched him come down the stairs. "You are a fine one that my husband hides up here," she said.

"Ma'am," Gabriel said, nodding his head to her as his mother had taught him.

"I am to feed you before you go. Sit down here. I'll cook an egg for you," she stated plainly, pointing to the table near the bar in the now-empty tavern.

He didn't know what to think but wasn't going to turn down a meal. He put his drum beside his chair and sat, watching the woman move toward the hearth that had already been warmed by a morning log. The woman cracked the egg on an iron skillet, which rested on a grate over the hot coals. She looked at him silently while she stirred the egg, scraping it onto a wooden plate next to a small piece of bread. "You'll be wanting something to drink? I will bring you some milk." The woman walked out the back door.

Gabriel finished his egg, when the woman brought in a cup of fresh milk, sat it down, and said, "I don't know what kind of spell you worked on Ben Daniels. You got him to pay for a room and for this hot food. You must be a good boy. Eat, eat!" The woman smiled now.

Gabriel felt better. He smiled back at the woman. She got up from the table and went to work wiping off tables. He finished his meal and said his thank-yous to the woman. She smiled again and waved goodbye as he walked through the door. Slinging his pack over his back, he put his hand in his pocket and felt his ring and the loose change the tavern owner had given him from his dinner the night before. He liked the feel of coins in his pocket. Jingling his change, he set off for King's Bridge.

He had his drum at his side and was trying not to make it too obvious that he was carrying the instrument as he approached the bridge. It was made of stone and wide and fairly long. He would have liked to stop and look over the edge at the Harlem River below, but he thought it would be best not to delay. So he walked briskly across with nobody else in sight. *So far, so good*, he thought. *This may be easier than I imagined.*

The thought had no sooner crossed his mind than he heard hoof beats up ahead on the road. He quickly darted to the north side and down an embankment under the bridge. The horses' hooves pounded overhead, echoing loudly in his ears. His heart raced, and his breath quickened. He waited, hoping no one had seen him. *What if Reverend Loring sends men out looking for me?* he thought. *What if the reverend told the loyalists in New York that I am a traitor?*

Gabriel tried to push back his fear, but he knew he would have to be cautious on the road. After waiting several minutes, he put his ear to the bottom of the bridge to listen for any sounds of approaching horses. The road above was silent. Cautiously, he climbed back up the embankment. Seeing no one, he ran north along the road, away from the bridge.

As he headed north through Yonkers, it seemed like he heard a horse with a wagon or carriage come beating and rattling along the road every thirty minutes. Each time, he was forced to dive into the grass or bushes along the side of the road and wait. When he emerged, he was a little bit dirtier, and his coat and pants had a few more burrs in them. He even had burrs stuck in his thick black hair.

Gabriel was tired of running off the road for cover in the thickets and bushes. *Surely all of these horses and carriages can't be loyalists or king's soldiers looking for a patriot to terrorize,* he thought. *In fact, it is not likely many redcoats would even be on this road. They can't get into Boston by land without running into the militia surrounding the city. They would have to use a boat, and if they have to go by boat, they would just board a ship at New York and sail to Boston.*

As the afternoon sun began to sink in the sky, Gabriel didn't hear an approaching traveler along the road for some time. Making good time now, he passed taverns at New Rochelle, Larchmont, and Mamaroneck. He saw a few farms off the road in the distance, with cattle grazing and men out working in the fields. As inviting as the taverns and farms appeared, he kept to the road.

He was just thinking about stopping for a quick rest, when he heard approaching hoof beats coming from behind. He began to head for a patch of tall and scruffy grass a few yards off the road, but, just as his foot left the rutted dirt path of the road, he changed his mind.

Instead he continued to walk alongside the edge, making sure he was out of the way of the approaching horses. The hoof beats began to grow a little louder now. He thought again of the advice that Ben Daniels gave him back at the tavern about taking to the bushes to avoid travelers. He couldn't make up his mind, and then, at the last minute, as the horses were now approaching loudly and quickly, he dove into some thick bushes beside the road.

He waited, panting now from the last-minute sprint. Strangely, he now heard nothing but his own breathing, no hoof beats trailing off into the distance—nothing at all. *Were the horses going at such a brisk pace that they've already passed out of earshot?* wondered Gabriel.

The abrupt silence made him uneasy, and he wondered if he should run further into the surrounding trees. Trying to calm himself, he took a deep breath. Dozens of riders had passed on horseback over the course of the day, and none of them had been out looking to capture him and take him back to New York. *This is nonsense,* he thought. *Why am I hiding?* He decided to go out and meet whoever might have stopped in the road.

Just as he was about to peek out of the bushes, he heard footsteps approaching and he was suddenly yanked from the bushes. The branches scraped and cut his face, and he was tossed down into the grass alongside the road. He looked up and saw a squat, stocky man standing over him. Dark eyes, framed by even darker fleshy rings, now stared down at him. He let out a gasp. This was Hannigan, Grimm's helper from the tavern.

A dark shadow of a man sat on horseback, looming over Gabriel and Hannigan. The rider's voice bellowed, "Well, well, well . . . look what we have here, Hannigan."

Gabriel squinted up at the rider in his mount. Bradford Grimm himself sat tall and ominous, peering down with a devilish grin upon his face. He still wore his faded red jacket, and his musket was strapped to the back of his saddle. Grimm shook his head and clucked his tongue. "What are you running from, lad?"

Gabriel was speechless.

"What's the matter, boy, cat got your tongue?" Hannigan laughed. His crooked yellow teeth snarled at Gabriel. "The only people who run from His Majesty's loyal subjects are those who have something to hide. So let's have a good look at you, now."

As Gabriel was now thrown to his feet, his mind began to race. Where was his sack? Where was his drum? Had Grimm or Hannigan seen either of these things yet? He still did not say a word to Hannigan, who was now roughly shaking him, as if to see whether anything loose might fall off of him.

"Let's have a look in those pockets." Gabriel felt the ring and the change he had in his pocket. He certainly did not want to hand over his ring, and, even though there wasn't much change, he didn't want to turn that over to Hannigan and Grimm, either.

"Hold on a minute, Hannigan," interrupted Grimm, still seated on his horse. "What's over there in the bushes?"

Forgetting about Gabriel's pockets, Hannigan wandered over to the bushes where Gabriel had dove in just a few minutes ago, and pulled out his sack and drum. Gabriel's heart pounded. Should he run? "Well, I'll be me mother's laddie, we caught ourselves a little drummer boy, Grimm." Hannigan held Gabriel's drum up high for all to see. "But where is the rest of your army, following along to the beat of your drum? Come to think of it, where are your drumsticks, drummer boy?" Hannigan laughed heartily at his own joke.

Grimm, however, sat motionless, recognition growing across his face. His fierce eyes beat down on Gabriel. "You're the boy from the King's Bridge Tavern. You were there. I saw you come in with your drum."

Hannigan's laugh trailed off. "Oh, yeah. I recognize him now. I told you we ought to ask him some questions when he came into the tavern. Remember?"

Grimm shot Hannigan a look of disgust. "Of course I remember, you half-wit! Hand me his pack!" commanded Grimm.

Gabriel's thoughts were spinning. His money was in that cloth pack. He couldn't lose it. He wouldn't be able to buy food. How could he make it to Boston with no food? Grimm clutched the bunched-up blanket that served as Gabriel's sack, his hand like a claw getting ready to rip into it.

Gabriel shouted, "No! Stop! I will give you all the money I have if you will only give me back my sack."

Hannigan chuckled up at Grimm, "What'ya think, Grimm? Maybe we ought to take all the coppers he has and the sack, too."

Ignoring Hannigan, Grimm gave Gabriel a long, curious look. "What's in the sack that you don't want us to see, drummer boy?"

Gabriel knew this was his only opportunity to get his sack of belongings back. His mind racing, he tried to think up some story about what was in his sack. Ben Daniels had told him to use his head in a situation like this. Maybe the pack was filled with gunpowder that was about to explode, or snakes full of poisonous venom.

Unable to think of a story that would convince them not to open the pack, he looked Bradford Grimm squarely in the eyes and relied on a truth. "There's a note from my mother in that sack. You see, she and my pa died of the pox about a year ago, and those words on that paper are the only thing I have to remember her by. I don't have many coppers, but I'll give it all to you if you only give my sack back with that note."

Gabriel put his hand in his pocket, felt the ring his mother had given him, and shifted it to the side. He pulled out the change and held it in front Hannigan and Grimm. It was just a couple of coppers.

Before Gabriel could say another word, Grimm took out a knife and cut away the string on his sack. Gabriel's heart sank. Grimm dumped out the contents of the sack onto the road. There fell his knife, his flask, his flint rock, and the note from his mother. The small pouch that held his money was missing. Gabriel looked in amazement. Where was his coin pouch?

Hannigan ran over to snatch up the knife, flint rock, and paper, when Grimm spoke up. "Hannigan, take his coppers for payment for using the King's Highway without permission, and leave his belongings."

Somewhat startled, Hannigan dropped Gabriel's things back to the ground. "But, sir," questioned Hannigan.

Grimm glared at Hannigan, daring him to say another word. Reluctantly, Hannigan kicked the contents that spilled out of Gabriel's pack to the side of the road, covering them with dirt.

"Boy," continued Grimm, in a commanding tone, "I know where you're going, and I know what you're going to do with that pitiful drum when you get there. You are headed north on this road to meet up with the rebels and traitors that call themselves a militia. I—and many others—stand ready to do whatever we must to defeat these rebels. At this very moment, I am upon urgent business from the royal governor of New York himself. I, therefore, unfortunately do not have time to transport you back to New York, where you would likely be tried and hanged as a traitor to the crown."

Grimm then paused, reached around to the back of his saddle, and pulled out his musket. Gabriel could only guess what was coming next. Would Grimm choose to stab him with the bayonet or put a musket ball through his head? He closed his eyes tightly, afraid that if he opened them, he might start weeping.

Grimm shouted. "Open your eyes, boy, when an official of the royal governor is speaking!" He pointed the musket down on Gabriel and spoke slowly. "You must turn around, return to New York, and give up your rebellious ways. You will never reach Boston. You have no coins, no food, and no gun, and the road up ahead is a wilderness. I will say this only once: if you choose to disobey my orders, *you will die*. You will either starve, fall ill, be devoured by a wild animal, shot by a bandit, or stopped by my fellow loyalists, who are within their rights to charge you as a traitor and string you up from the nearest tree. Do I make myself clear?"

Gabriel only nodded.

"Very well," said Grimm, gathering up his reins. Hannigan snatched the coins from Gabriel's hand and threw his drum back into the thorny bushes as hard as he could. He then pushed Gabriel down into the road and held his face tightly against the dirt. Leaning down, he put his hot, stinking breath next to Gabriel's face and said, "I hope you heard what Mr. Grimm said. If it was up to me, I'd run you through right here and now."

Hannigan stood up and kicked him hard in the ribs. Gabriel felt as though a spike had been driven into his side. The air was forced from his lungs in a loud gasp, and he writhed in pain.

"Hurry up, Hannigan," shouted Grimm.

Climbing back on his horse, Hannigan left Gabriel groaning in the road. The loyalists rode off, leaving a trail of dust that began to settle on Gabriel's already-dirty coat.

Gabriel began to lift himself off the ground and stood in the road, motionless. He tried to comprehend what just happened. He grabbed his bruised side, sorry for the pain he felt, but now he felt more the patriot than he ever had before. He was more determined than ever to stand up and march north.

He gathered up his belongings, and with a pain still stinging his side, he shook out his blanket to remove the dust. There was a large hole ripped down the middle of the blanket. He immediately threw it down and ran over to the bushes where Hannigan found his sack. There, lying on the ground next to the thorny bush that had slashed his face, was his coin pouch. He could not believe his eyes. A thorn must have torn a hole in his blanket when Hannigan had pulled it from the bushes, and the pouch had fallen out. A sense of relief came over him. He picked up the small pouch and kissed it. "Thank you, God. Thank you," he muttered.

He remembered Ben's words: *I do not believe there are many things in this life that happen just by chance.* What other explanation could there be for these loyalists not finding his coins?

With his aching side still shooting pain, he needed to rest. He picked up his drum and tramped through the bushes to find a place to lie down. Once he did, the exhaustion from the day's turmoil overwhelmed him. He thought about what had happened. Between his pain and his restless thoughts, sleep was elusive yet again. He kept returning to the same question over and over: *Why was I spared?*

Finally, unable to find an answer, he gave in to his exhaustion and fell asleep among the bushes.

★ 5 ★

BATTLE BREWING

Gabriel woke up with soreness from the kick to his side and a grumbling sound coming from his stomach. It was damp and dark out, with a thick fog shrouding the moon and stars. His stomach growled again, yet he had nothing to eat to satisfy his growing hunger. The only thing he could do was pack up his things and start walking. At least it was dark and foggy. No chance of being spotted by more loyalists.

He headed back to the road and slowly began to move his stiff and sore muscles, hoping they would limber up as he went along. He had no idea how long he had slept or what time of night it was. He only knew that he was hungry.

To forget his hunger, Gabriel began to think again about what had happened to him that afternoon with Grimm. He was thankful his coin pouch had fallen from his sack, but he was mad at himself for letting the crazed loyalists get hold of him in the first place. The pain in his side reminded him of his mistake. *If only I'd taken cover sooner,* he thought.

Then he remembered that Hannigan told him they stopped because they took notice of his running. If he had just stood by his decision to continue walking alongside the road, then Grimm and Hannigan might have ridden past without stopping. It was his indecision that just about ended his journey to Boston, and he knew it. He spoke to himself in the cool, foggy night air, "I have got to be able to make up my mind and stick with it."

Gabriel's stomach growled again, and his mind quickly returned to his hunger. Walking on, he saw a dim light off in the distance. With the thick fog blurring his vision, he wasn't sure how far away it was. He left the path and headed toward it. As he stepped through the tall grass alongside the road, small beads of rain began pelting him. He picked up his pace, but it seemed the faster he walked, the harder the rain came down. By the time he could see the outline of a house with a faint candle in the window, the rain was pouring down.

He approached the house with caution and carefully stepped onto the front porch. A board creaked, and he was about to turn and run, but nobody came to the door. Slowly and carefully, he peeked in through the candle-lit window. Except for the candle, which was about to burn out, there were no other lights inside. *Whoever lives here is probably asleep,* thought Gabriel, *and would not appreciate me knocking on their door to ask for some food.*

He looked around and saw a small barn not too far from the house. He decided to head for the barn to find a place to sleep out of the rain and wait until morning to ask for some food. It was hard to walk away from the house, with the thought of food sitting in a pantry inside, but he made up his mind and was going to stick with it. He left the cover of the porch and briskly walked to the barn. The barn door was unlocked, so he went inside. It was dark—so dark he couldn't see his hand in front of his face.

Not knowing what animals might be in the barn, he felt his way along the door to the wall. He then felt stall boards. A horse whinnied, and Gabriel felt its warm breath on his hand. "It's all right, I'm just looking for a place to sleep," he said to the horse.

A horse could be very useful, he realized. It was night, the barn was unlocked, and he could easily lead it out of the barn and ride off down the road. "No," Gabriel said to himself. "I may have to tell some lies to get to Boston, but I will not steal to get there." He could not bear the thought of some poor farmer waking up to find his horse gone and no way to plow his fields.

He looked around. His eyes had started to adjust to the blackness, and he spotted a pile of hay in the middle of the barn. Walking carefully to the pile, he began to arrange some on the floor for a bed. Raindrops pelted the top of the roof. He knew the peaceful sound would soon put him to sleep. He laid his head down on the hay and shut his eyes.

Suddenly, the barn door flew open with a tremendous crash and a blinding light. It was so bright, Gabriel had to put his arm over his eyes. A shot rang out, and then something hard was thrust into his chest. Taking his arm away from his squinting eyes, he saw a man with a lantern standing over him, poking him in the chest with a musket. The man shouted at him, "State your business! Why are you trespassing in my barn?"

"I was only looking for a dry place to lie down, sir," Gabriel trembled.

"This here barn ain't no hotel and my house ain't no tavern, so get out before I shoot ya full of lead," shouted the man.

Gabriel stood, his clothes still soaking wet and water dripping from his hair. He picked up his sack and drum and headed for the barn door. Just as he put his hand on the door, he heard the man say, "Wait." He thought about making a run for it through the barn door and into the darkness but, instead, decided to stop.

"I can't let you stay here," said the man. "His Majesty's soldiers are boarding a boat just off the coast only a few miles from us. Word is, they've been inclined to search houses along the road and take things they claim to need. I don't want them to come into this barn and find me harboring a runaway who, by the looks of him, might be on his way to Boston to fight."

By now, Gabriel was not surprised this man had figured out where he was going. Everyone else he had met knew what he was up to. "I'll leave then, sir. I don't want you to face trouble because of me."

"Stay put, lad," said the man, holding the lantern up higher to see his face.

The man had a hard and weathered face and grizzled gray hair. Without saying another word, he slid past Gabriel with his gun still at his side. The man's lantern bounced and swayed up to the house. Once he could no longer see the man, Gabriel stepped out through the barn door. He didn't like the look of him, and the thought of disappearing into the darkness raced through Gabriel's mind once again.

He again recalled the events of the day before. He thought about Bradford Grimm and the beaten boy in the tavern. Could this old man be another loyalist in disguise? Still, if the man were going to turn him in or do any harm, he would have done so already. Less than certain he was making the right choice, Gabriel stayed, as the man told him.

He sat in the dark barn, waiting. After some time, he gazed through the barn to the house. Nothing. He began to doubt his decision to stay. Maybe the man had gone to alert nearby soldiers of his presence?

He listened to the rain pelting the roof of the barn. It seemed a little less peaceful now. Again, he looked through the darkness of the barn to the rain outside. About an hour passed when he wondered, *What could be taking him so long? Perhaps I should go.* But just as he was readying to leave, the barn door squeaked open, and the man entered with his lantern in one hand and something else in the other.

"Take this with you," said the man softly. He held out a towel-wrapped bundle.

Gabriel took it from the man and slowly opened the towel a bit to see what was inside. The smell of food (biscuits and some ham) hit him like an ocean wave. It was so overwhelming he nearly lost his composure and shoveled the food into his mouth right then and there. Instead, he took a deep breath and looked up at the man. "Thank you, sir."

"You can thank me by getting out of my barn, laddie," barked the man. But then, through the rough scowl on his weathered face, he smiled at Gabriel.

Gabriel picked up his bundle and took a step for the door. As he did, the man suddenly spoke. "Laddie, my son has gone north to Boston to fight. Samuel O'Connor's his name. I tried to keep him from going. Damn foolishness, I told him. Foolishness. He wouldn't listen to me. I will give you the same warning I gave him: stay with your family. Leave the fighting to others. They say there's going to be a great battle soon, just outside Boston. You know what that tells me, don't ya? Men are going to die, that's what that means. Go home, lad," said the man in a shaky voice.

"I can't go home, sir. I haven't got one."

There was a moment of silence between them as they just stared at one another.

"Then go with God, laddie. And be careful."

"I will, sir. And thank you for the food." Gabriel turned and went into the wet darkness.

★ 6 ★

80 CANNON

Gabriel awoke from a short, restless sleep under a tall pine tree with thick branches that shielded him from the rain. His woolen coat was soaked with the heavy morning dew, and it was cold against his skin. Shivering, he drew his knees in up under his chin as he sat on the ground, trying to warm up.

He reflected on the kindness shown to him the night before. Perhaps he reminded the old man of his own son leaving to go to Boston. It made him think of his own father again. He wished his father had been there to see him off to fight for freedom, but, then again, he probably wouldn't have gone if his parents were still alive. He couldn't begin thinking that way again, though. He had already wasted too many hours thinking about what life should have been like for him, instead of how it was. He had finally come to accept his circumstances and make the best of what he'd been given

At the moment, it seemed like he had been given a lot. The thought of the biscuits and ham consumed him once again. He had plenty left for a good breakfast. He set the towel down on the bed of pine needles and couldn't keep from stuffing his mouth so full of food he could hardly swallow.

After eating almost every morsel, it dawned on him he should save some of the food for later. Reluctantly, he folded what was left of the meal back into the towel and stuffed it into his rolled-up sack. The sky was still dark, with no sign of a rising sun, so he laid back down, though he was no longer sleepy.

He thought about starting a fire to warm up and dry out, but he was afraid it would draw too much attention. The best plan was to find his way back to the road and get moving. Walking would help warm him up, and with any luck, the clouds would give way to some sunshine. As soon as he saw the sun start to rise, Gabriel stood, picked up his belongings, and stepped out from under the large pine tree that had been his shelter for the night.

The sunrise gave some light to the gray clouds above, but Gabriel still didn't know which way to go. Where was the road? There was no clear way to figure out where he had come from the night before. It had been too dark, foggy, and rainy to have seen much of anything. Still, having heard that soldiers were lurking about, he wanted to get going.

He noticed a stream of smoke wafting into the air back in the direction of the home of the man who had fed him last night. Getting his bearings, he headed in the direction he thought the road would be. After walking a long time, he mumbled to himself, "I hope I haven't headed the wrong way. I don't remember it taking me this long to reach that barn last night."

He kept on going in the same direction toward the east. Just to the north, he saw a hill that hadn't been visible in the dark. *I'll climb to the top*, he thought. *From there I'll be able to see the land around me.*

When he first noticed it, the hill looked small. But as he neared, Gabriel realized the climb would be more of a challenge than at first sight. The slopes were steep and rocky, but he was determined to reach the top. He hoped to be able to see the road from there.

The lower rise of the hill was a meadow with a few trees scattered about. Wildflowers had started to bloom, and their blossoms dotted the green grass with purple, pink, and yellow. As he neared the halfway point, the slope became much steeper and the grass gave way to rocky soil. He slung his drum and sack over his back and began to climb. With each step, his foot slipped on the rocky surface. He grabbed hold of trees and roots to pull his way up. By now, he was breathing hard. The top was in sight, but to reach it, he would have to make one final push over a larger boulder jutting out from the side of the hill. Lying down on his stomach, he crawled up and over this last obstacle.

Once he reached the top, all he could do was lie on his back and look up at the sky. His arms and legs burned as though they were on fire, and he felt as if he would never catch his breath. The gray rain clouds were beginning to give way to puffy white clouds, with streaks of interwoven blue. Encouraged by the thought of approaching sunshine, Gabriel rose to his feet and looked out.

The view both captivated and terrified Gabriel. He hadn't realized he was so close to the sound. He could see the tops of tall trees—oaks and pines, maples and spruce. They seemed to stretch out all around, covering the land all the way to the water. But anchored there just beyond the shoals were two grand ships.

These ships were flying the flag with the king's colors in the canton with a white ensign and St. George's cross atop their main masts, the colors flapping briskly in the wind. He squinted now, trying to see the details of the ships. They were large, set deep in the water, and appeared to have many openings along the sides, much like windows. He thought for a minute, and then it dawned on him what the openings were. Cannon ports. These were ships-of-the-line.

While Gabriel had seen plenty of English merchant ships flying the British Red Ensign sail into New York Harbor, he'd never seen ships like these. He tried to count the openings, but he always lost count at about forty or so. If there were forty cannon on one side of the ship, there would have to be forty on the other side, as well. "Eighty cannon," he uttered in amazement.

He remembered reading a book about Royal Navy ships in his father's bookstore and always wanted to see one in person, but now, as he looked out at those two massive ships, his heart began to sink. "They must be headed for Boston!" he said out loud.

Gabriel spied a much smaller boat that was being rowed out from the docks. He could also see sailors raising and lowering the oars of the boat. The man he had met last night was right. They must be loading up their ships with all available soldiers to send them to Boston. *There is only one reason to put all your soldiers in one place,* thought Gabriel. *Because you are getting ready to attack.*

The thought of the British attacking the militia around Boston without him there to help in the fight was almost unbearable. "The road . . . I have got to find the road," Gabriel gasped. He took his eyes off the ships and scanned the area. He could not see the road anywhere until he finally looked nearly straight down. There, right at the bottom of the hill, lay a winding strip of dirt road. If he had gone just a few hundred yards farther instead of climbing the hill, he would have been back to the road long ago. Still, if he hadn't climbed the hill, he wouldn't have been able to see the awesome scene laid out before him.

He took it in one last time before turning his eyes back down to the road, carefully looking for redcoats moving along its path and seeing none. As he looked to the east, he spotted a small village in the distance. He could easily reach it in a day's walk.

Gabriel was more determined than ever to travel to Boston as fast as he could. It was nearly the end of April, and the British were on the move. He quickly descended the hill, almost sliding straight down along some of the steepest ravines and gullies, grasping at trees and roots to slow him down. When he reached the bottom, he was covered in a brownish mud. But he didn't care what he looked like. He was back on the road and heading toward Boston.

Even though Gabriel was still wet and now filthy, as well, it felt good to be heading in the right direction again. There was little traffic on the road, and by high noon, he reached the group of houses he saw from the hill. He left his drum covered under some bushes on the edge of the village and walked through the streets, as if he knew exactly where he was going. He decided it was best not to gawk around and wander aimlessly, raising suspicions in observers' minds. *If you do not look suspicious*, he concluded, *you are less likely to be bothered.*

While he did his best to look like he knew where he was going, he did nothing to mask his muddy, ratty appearance. He strolled confidently down the street, but more than one of the villagers stopped in their tracks to stare at him as he walked. He ignored the attention.

He noticed a sign above one of the buildings that read, "Fairfield Food & Drink." He began walking toward the building when a man sitting in a rocking chair just outside the door shouted, "You been wrestling with the pigs, boy?"

"Who, me?" retorted Gabriel.

"Yes, you. I saw you coming from all the way down the street. I think half the town noticed you. I've seen some dirt in my day, but I would have say you're 'bout the muddiest-looking wretch I've seen."

Gabriel now looked down at his pants and coat and realized what a spectacle he really was.

"Come inside," said the man in the rocking chair, getting up to stand. "I've got a fire going. You can take those wet and muddy things you call clothes off to dry."

Grateful to get out of sight, Gabriel stepped inside the building. *So much for not drawing attention*, he thought. Still, the man did not ask him any questions about who he was or where he was going. He just let him dry out his clothes a bit and buy something to eat and drink.

"I've got a spare room if you need a place to sleep tonight, son," the man offered.

"Thank you, sir," replied Gabriel, "but I need to get going. I've rested here long enough in front of your fire. I have many more miles ahead of me before I reach my destination."

"Very well," said the man. "Looks like more rain rolling in, though. You might want to reconsider."

Gabriel was already putting his coat back on and picking up his pack. "I'll stay dry, thank you." He headed out the door and waved. He turned as if he was heading on east, but once he was out of sight, he ducked into a back alley and hurried to the spot where he'd left his drum. He found it just as he'd left it, and he was glad to have it back. He was sure this was the only way he was going to be allowed to join the militia, even if he didn't have any drumsticks.

Back on the road again, Gabriel was determined to make as much progress as he could. He thought about reaching the militia around Boston and asking for Nathaniel Greene, just as Ben Daniels had told him to. He wondered if the ships in the sound had raised anchor yet. *When will they reach Boston Harbor? Or were the soldiers from the ships already on the ground marching against the militia?* These thoughts quickened his pace.

Distracted by his thoughts of reaching Boston, he hardly noticed when the pitter-patter of rain began to fall on his head. The rain quickly turned into a downpour. He ran for cover under a large oak tree, but the rain was coming down hard, and the wind was whipping through the tree so much that the oak did little to shelter him. His woolen coat was soaked again. Soon, the approaching night air would become cooler. He knew he was in for a long night. He thought of the fire he had sat by earlier that afternoon, and it warmed his thoughts.

That was it—a fire! Gabriel went to gather some small branches and pine needles. He stacked them in a pile and took his flint rock from his pouch. Then he struck his flint with his knife. Sparks flew, but no fire took hold. He struck again and again, but it was simply too wet. With this rain-soaked wood, he wouldn't have a fire tonight.

Gabriel leaned back against the base of the oak tree and hung his head. As he did, the cold rain dripped from his black hair onto the ground. He watched it drip, wishing he had stayed in the room the innkeeper offered him. He could be sitting by a warm fire right now, but, instead, he was here in the cold, pouring rain with night falling around him. Uncomfortable as he was, he tried to go to sleep. Dwelling on thoughts of a warm fire would do him no good. Instead, he tried to think about how good his full stomach felt. With the thought of a satisfied belly, he finally fell asleep in the cold rain.

★ 7 ★
NEW HAVEN

Gabriel awoke cold, stiff, and wet. A gray drizzle filled the sky, and, at first, it was hard for him to tell if it was day or night. With his eyes blurred by the dripping rain, he wiped his sleeve over his face and looked out at the world. He stood and stretched but soon realized stretching would not make him feel any better.

In fact, the more he moved, the worse he felt. He blamed his lack of energy on his side, which still ached from Hannigan's kick. He grabbed his pack, left the tree, and wandered back out to the road. As he moved, he felt a funny twinge in his throat. Still, he pressed on for most of the day in the continuous cold rain. He had to reach Boston soon.

With no sun, he had no idea what time it was. He felt as if he had been walking forever. Suddenly, he felt really warm. The warmth felt good at first, but then it seemed to zap every ounce of energy left in him. He stopped a moment on the road. As he did, the warmth disappeared and he shook uncontrollably. He was so cold he felt paralyzed. He dropped to the ground and tried to warm himself.

Gabriel realized he was ill. Could he make it back to the innkeeper whose fire he had sat by the day before? No. He would only go forward. He had to press on to get to Boston before the ships.

He pulled himself up off the muddy road and began to walk again. His head began to pound. He could hardly keep his eyes open, but when he shut them, his mind began to spin.

All along his route, he'd wanted to avoid other travelers, until now. He would have rejoiced to see anyone coming up the road with a horse and carriage, but no one came. Gabriel slogged on through the muddy road. He had to concentrate on putting one foot in front of the other. He only hoped that he was headed in the right direction. Not even having the strength to hold up his head, he began to stumble. His drum and pack of belongings hung alongside him, dragging through the mud.

Gabriel's foot hit a rock or branch in the mud, and he fell. He was so weak, he couldn't even bring his arm up to help break his fall. As his face hit the mud, he thought for a brief moment how cool it felt. He didn't think he could get up. He didn't want to get up. He couldn't even muster the strength to raise his head out of the mud. Would he end up like his parents, unable to recover from a sudden, overwhelming sickness?

Gabriel stretched out his arm and felt something hard. Was this what he tripped over? He felt it with his hand. It was

a stone of some sort. He could feel letters etched in the surface. Was it a gravestone? Had he stumbled into a cemetery?
How fitting, he thought.

His curiosity sparked enough strength that he was able to
raise his head. Peering through the murky rain and his dangling wet hair, he pulled his eyes closer to the etching in the
stone. He made out the writing. N-E-W H-A-V-E-N.

New Haven. That's just what I need, thought Gabriel, *a new
haven out of this rain and sickness.* He saw some more writing . . .
1 M-I-L-E.

New Haven one mile.

"One mile . . . one mile." Mumbling the words to himself
over and over again, he finally comprehended the meaning
of the stone marker he just tripped over. It was a mile marker
along the Boston Post Road, and it was only one mile to the
town of New Haven, Connecticut.

Only one mile. I can't give up when I'm so close. Gabriel slowly
pulled himself up. He grasped hold of the marker to pull himself to his feet, tugged at his drum and pack, and stumbled
back onto the road. Through all this, the rain continued, but
it didn't matter to him. He could have been walking through
the bottom of the ocean or the driest of deserts. He only had
one thing in mind: making it one more mile.

With blurred vision, Gabriel walked on senselessly. He
thought he heard something up ahead. It sounded like voices,
but he was unsure of anything now. Then he saw the blurry,

rain-soaked vision of a building ahead. A house? He careened up to the door and knocked once with every last ounce of strength he could muster. He slid down alongside the door and waited. As he slid down, he prayed the person who answered the door would not be a loyalist. He shut his eyes and leaned against the door.

He felt his head begin to fall as the door opened. Helplessly, he fell across the doorstep. He looked up, only able to open his blurry eyes halfway, seeing what looked like a girl standing over him.

"Oh my!" she gasped. The girl dragged him into the house and shut the door to keep out the wind and the rain. Gabriel was barely conscious now. He tried to speak, but he could not form the words.

"Constance," the girl shouted to a smaller girl, "stoke the fire. We need to warm this boy up." Out of the corner of his half-open eyes, Gabriel saw a small girl run over to the fire. A few years younger than Gabriel, she had dark black hair that came down to her shoulders. She threw some pieces of wood on the fire and poked it with an iron rod.

Flames soon began to jump up, and Constance declared, "Malinda, the fire's going now." Both girls pulled Gabriel up to a chair that was close to the hearth. Next, they pulled off his coat and took off his shoes. Although Gabriel was grateful, this kind attention did nothing to increase his strength. Malinda, the older of the two girls, placed her hand on his forehead. She, too, had dark black hair, but it flowed down longer than her sister's. He was able to see her dark eyes and her skin, tanned by the sun. She wore a simple linen dress and appeared to be as tall as Gabriel. "By the grace of the good Lord, this boy is burning up with fever," Malinda said. "Father won't be back until dark, but this boy needs help now."

"We could go fetch the druggist," said Constance.

"Yes, Mr. Arnold. With Doctor Brown gone to Boston, he'll have to do. He'll be able to give the boy some medicine," replied Malinda. "Constance, put your cloak on, and run to Mr. Arnold's shop. I do hope he is there. You know how he travels about."

"Yes. I will run as fast as I can." Constance pulled on her woolen cloak and ran through the door at full speed.

Even though Gabriel was seated next to the fire, he was still shivering and too weak to speak. He gazed into the flames of the fire—orange, red, and then blue—then closed his eyes. The flames continued to dance in his mind as he began to dream. Bradford Grimm was now standing before him. Grimm, instead of Malinda and Constance, had opened the door for Gabriel. In place of his faded red jacket, he was now arrayed in the bright red colors of the king's own soldiers. The fire glinted and gleamed off his uniform's brass buttons and silver trimmings.

He picked Gabriel up, shook him, and threw him across the room. Gabriel lay curled on the floor when his parents suddenly appeared through the door. Grimm rushed at them, knocking his parents down. He drew some rope from his jacket and tied their hands and feet. Then he forced them to stand against a wall. He took his musket from his shoulder and raised it at the couple.

All Gabriel could see was Grimm's bayonet, with its shiny glow of sharpened steel gleaming at the end of the musket. Grimm drew it closer and closer. Then, suddenly, a British ship came bursting through the door, blasting its cannons. The whole room was shaking.

"Boy, boy . . . BOY! Can you hear me?"

Gabriel looked up, expecting to see a room filled with cannon smoke but instead saw the face of the girl who had let him in. He was able to nod his head once.

"Constance has returned with Mr. Arnold. He has brought you some medicine."

A finely dressed man stood beside Gabriel and looked him over. "Boy, I'm going to need you to drink something. I'll tell you now, it will not taste good. If you spit it out, I will not give you more. Without this medicine you will remain very ill and may die. Do you understand me?"

Gabriel nodded slightly.

"Malinda, do you have any wine for me to mix with the quinine medicine?" asked Mr. Arnold. "I could mix it with water, but it has such a horribly bitter taste that masking it with some wine usually helps it go down."

"Yes," replied Malinda. "I will run to the cellar and fetch you some."

Malinda returned with a bottle of wine and a cup. Mr. Arnold took the bottle and poured some of the wine into the cup. Then, pulling a small paper envelope from his pocket, Mr. Arnold used his knife to cut a small slit and tapped the envelope three times on the edge of the cup. A fine white powder fell through the slit and into the cup. "A spoon to stir this, please," Mr. Arnold requested.

Constance returned with a spoon and, with a few stirs, the mixture was ready. "Help prop his head up, girls. It is very important he drinks all of this." Mr. Arnold held the cup to Gabriel's lips. "Remember what I said. Down the hatch, all of it."

The quinine and wine slowly dribbled into Gabriel's mouth. As weak as he was, he immediately felt the urge to spew this bitter drink from his mouth. But he sent the mixture to the back of his throat, trying to keep it from touching his tongue, and swallowed until the whole cup was gone.

"Well done, my boy, well done," exclaimed Mr. Arnold. "A tough one, girls. I give good odds he will recover from the fever if he is able to stomach that much quinine without spilling a drop." Mr. Arnold looked at Malinda and Constance. "Wherever did this boy come from?"

"We do not know," responded Malinda. "There was just a knock on the door, and he fell in when I opened it. He had these things with him." Malinda pointed to Gabriel's sack and drum, which were placed in the corner.

Mr. Arnold looked at the drum. "I have my guesses, at least, about where this boy is headed and what he wishes to do when he gets there."

At that moment, the door to the house opened. Malinda and Constance ran to the man standing at the door, himself rather wet, and hugged him.

"Oh, Father, come sit down by the fire. We have so much to tell you."

The girls' father stepped inside and said stiffly, "Why, Mr. Benedict Arnold, I didn't expect to see you here. Is someone sick?"

"Well, yes. Young Constance came to the apothecary and said a boy had come by with a horrible fever and you were gone. He needed medicine straight away."

The girls' father stepped toward the fire and saw Gabriel in the chair.

"I gave him some quinine. He is a strong lad. Took it all down. He has been toting a drum around. I do not know this for a fact, but I would guess he is a drummer boy, probably trying to join up with the militia gathering around Boston. He must have walked some distance. He certainly has been out in the cold rain for the past couple of days."

"A drummer boy?" questioned the girls' father. "Well, God bless the lad. We will do our best to help him recover."

"I will leave this packet of quinine. Give him two doses a day. The girls saw me mix it. Just do the same as I did, Malinda," Mr. Arnold told the girl.

Constance and Malinda nodded at Benedict Arnold.

Their father stepped to the table and laid down three dead rabbits. "Rabbit stew!" exclaimed Constance. "Can Mr. Arnold stay for dinner, Father?"

Her father looked awkwardly at Constance and then at Arnold, but before he could say anything, Arnold broke the uncomfortable silence. "No, no, thank you, Constance. I have to get back to the store. There is much to get done before my own departure to aid in our fight against the king. I have word from General Israel Putnam that I am to organize our Connecticut men to go to Boston."

"Maybe if the boy recovers quickly, you can take him with your Connecticut men," said Malinda.

"That may be, but what if your father wants to keep the boy here to help in the fields this spring? Besides, he is a rather handsome-looking chap, don't you think?" Arnold gave a wink and a smile to Malinda, which made her blush. "I will consider taking him with me. No doubt that I probably have another week's worth of preparation and will certainly stop by to check in on the lad before I go."

With that, Benedict Arnold put on his coat and hat, gave a short bow to the girls, and stepped to the door. "Good evening," he said as he gently pulled the door shut behind him.

The girls' father turned and looked at them with thoughtful eyes. "There goes a man full of ambition. Ambition which I pray will be used wholeheartedly to fight the redcoats."

★ 8 ★
HOPE

Gabriel slowly opened his eyes to a blinding light piercing through the room. Where was he? He remembered pulling himself up along the side of the road, stumbling through the rain, and falling down. He could remember no more.

With his eyes squinting from the brightness, he could tell he was looking out a window with sunshine beaming in through the panes of glass. It was the brightest sunshine he had ever seen, filling the little room where he lay in a small bed covered in thick quilts. He slowly looked around the room. Thick books rested on a bookshelf along one wall. A chair sat next to his bed, with a small wash pan and a towel sitting beside it.

He heard steps. He looked at the door, his senses still trying to awaken. He certainly did not expect a pretty girl with an angelic smile to walk in holding a cup with steam wafting from the top. For a moment, he faintly recognized her.

The girl stopped suddenly when she saw that Gabriel's eyes were open. "Well, I didn't expect to see you awake," she said softly. "You have been stirring quite a bit ever since your fever broke. I went to fetch you some hot broth. It will be much easier to get it down you now that you're awake." She paused, giving him a moment to respond, but he remained silent. "What's the matter? Can't you talk?"

Gabriel started to say something, but his lips felt like they were glued together. Once he got them separated, his tongue felt like a lead weight in his mouth. He realized that it must have been several days since he had spoken.

"Thhhhannk yooouuu," Gabriel finally slurred. "Whhhaat's yoouuurrr name?"

"Malinda," replied the girl.

"Hhoww lonngg have I been here?" asked Gabriel. The words started to come a little easier now.

"Almost a week. It's the first of May. I doubt you'll remember much of it, though. You were very sick. Now, enough of this chitter-chatter. You need to drink this soup before it gets cold. The warmth will help you feel better."

He was too weak to argue with Malinda, so he took the cup in his hands, feeling its warmth. Slowly, he touched it to his lips and took a sip. The warm broth filled him from the inside out. He took another sip, and then, feeling his strength being renewed from the nourishment, he drank the rest down in one gulp.

Malinda looked on in shock. "Well, I guess that hit the spot. I suppose I will excuse your lack of manners in guzzling that soup down like a pig eats its slop. After all, I do expect you are hungry. I think Constance just pulled a loaf of bread from the oven. I will bring you some."

"And some more broth. Please, miss," requested Gabriel.

"And some more broth. I am glad you like it." Malinda smiled warmly.

As Malinda turned to leave the room, Gabriel felt an overwhelming sense of gratefulness over how this girl had cared for him in his sickness. He has not seen a warm, embracing smile for a long time, let alone from a pretty girl his age.

Before long, Malinda returned with bread, soup, and another, smaller girl. "You must be Constance," he said, looking at the girl as she gave a blushing giggle with a dimpled smile from behind Malinda. He took the food and tried as best he could not to devour it as if he were a pig, this time aware both girls were watching him.

"I have to get my strength back so I can get back on the road. I would like to leave tonight."

No sooner had he said those words than he remembered how foolish he had been to leave the innkeeper's fire and venture out into the pouring rain. He had been impatient, and he knew it. He had almost died from his lack of patience. Yet, here he was again, failing to recognize his weakness. It was ridiculous to think he would somehow be able to return on his journey when he had not moved a muscle in a week.

Malinda looked at Gabriel. "Well, you have yet to properly introduce yourself by even telling me your name, and now you want to get up and leave. You are free to go anytime you like, taking your ill manners with you. But I suggest you stay here until you are at least strong enough to walk."

He appreciated the strength in Malinda's words and knew she was right. "My name is Gabriel, Gabriel Cooper, and I am traveling from New York to Boston. I will heed your advice and stay here until my strength returns, and I am very grateful for your kindness, hospitality, and all you have done for me."

Malinda smiled again and took the empty cup from his hands. "That's much better, Gabriel Cooper." Then, turning to her sister, "Constance, will you please go tell Father our mystery guest is named Gabriel Cooper, and he is awake?"

Constance disappeared and a few minutes later came back through the door with a ruddy, tall man. He sat down next to Gabriel.

"Well, I am glad to see you've made it, son. I had my doubts there for awhile, but we kept giving you Mr. Arnold's medicine and praying the good Lord would renew your health," said the man. "My daughter tells me you are called Gabriel Cooper and are from New York. I am Thomas Fleming, and I know you have met my daughters, Malinda and Constance. Now, you may not want me asking all of these questions, but I cannot delay. There may be people wanting to know where you are. Why have you left New York? Are you running away from your parents?"

Gabriel thought about the question for a moment. Technically he was running away from the Lorings, but the Lorings were not his parents, and so he plainly replied, "No, sir."

"The least you can do, after all we have done for you, is to tell us the truth," said Mr. Fleming softly but sternly. "Young boys such as yourself do not leave home without reason, son."

"I am telling you the truth, sir. I am not running away from my parents. They both died from the pox over a year ago. I do not have any family, so I left New York to join the militia gathering outside of Boston to fight for our freedom. I have a drum and am going to be a drummer boy." Gabriel had no idea if Mr. Fleming was a Tory or a patriot, but he knew he was about to find out.

He heard a soft whining sound after he finished. He looked over and saw Constance weeping softly in the corner of the small room.

"Don't cry," said Malinda, patting Constance on the back.

Gabriel wondered what he said to make the little girl cry. Mr. Fleming bowed his head slightly, almost whispering to Gabriel, "The girls lost their mother . . . my wife . . . from illness about a year ago. I'm sure your mentioning the death of your parents has brought back memories for them both. It's been very hard on them, especially young Constance. They've had to become the women who run the house, instead of just my little girls. There's not a day goes by that I don't think about their mother, and I know the same is true for them. I cannot imagine what it'd be like if they lost me, too. My heart goes out to you, Master Gabriel. I wish there was something I could do."

"Sir, you have already saved my life, and for that I owe you much more than can ever be paid," replied Gabriel.

"I can't say I had much of a hand in it. It was my girls, Mr. Benedict Arnold, and God's handiwork that saved you, son."

Just then, a knock came at the front door, and Mr. Fleming rose from Gabriel's side to answer it. Mr. Fleming returned with a man neatly dressed in a blue uniform, wearing shiny black boots and a cocked hat. The man removed his hat from his head and gave a slight bow to Malinda and Constance. "Ladies," he said in a soft but deep voice, "I see you have cared well for our patriot patient. You must have followed my directions extremely well." Mr. Arnold sat down next to Gabriel. "And how *are* you, young master drummer boy who is headed to Boston?"

Gabriel was in awe of the man's spotless appearance. He thought for a moment about how this man knew he had a drum and was headed to Boston, but before he could speak, Mr. Fleming said, "Captain Benedict Arnold is the druggist who brought over the quinine to bring down your fever. He's a merchant here in New Haven and has been all over the world sailing his ships. Now he is rounding up Connecticut men to go to Boston."

Gabriel's heart jumped at this news. *An officer who's taking men to Boston . . .* "Can I go with you to Boston, sir?" He started to move out of the bed, looking directly into Captain Arnold's eyes.

"Now, now," replied Captain Arnold, "I would say that you're in no condition to travel to Boston at the moment, but I'm not leaving right away. I will check back the day before I go and see if you're up to traveling. That means you better listen to what Misses Malinda and Constance tell you and get plenty of rest."

"I will, sir. Yes, sir. Don't worry, I will be better by then, sir, I know I will." Gabriel was speaking distinctly now, excited, a rush of adrenaline coursing through him. It seemed a giant weight had been lifted from his shoulders. The thought of being back out on the road again by himself seemed almost more than he could bear. But if he could travel beside men who had guns to hunt game, fires to sit by at night, and maybe even a tent to sleep under, there was hope. No matter what, he had to regain his strength. He would be ready to go with Captain Arnold to Boston.

★ 9 ★

THE TURN NORTH

Captain Arnold left Gabriel in the best spirits he had been in since he left New York. Mr. Fleming cleaned and repaired his drum with new rope and a new calfskin head. He made a leather sling that fit him, too. Malinda and Constance continued to care for Gabriel, who had started taking walks to regain his strength. On the fifth day since his fever broke, he got up from his bed and stepped outside. This day, he knew, might be his last with the Flemings. The word in town was Benedict Arnold was getting ready to leave for Boston. Gabriel took a deep breath of fresh air and felt more alive than he had ever felt. He even asked Mr. Fleming if he could help him split wood, but Mr. Fleming told him he needed to rest.

Gabriel spent that afternoon walking about the small Fleming farm, just on the edge of New Haven, Connecticut, with Malinda as his guide. The farm had a cow, some chickens, and, of course, a large field that had recently been plowed.

"We'll be doing our spring planting soon," said Malinda. "Father likes to wait until later to plant corn, but we've already planted potatoes and beans."

"I wish I could stay and help. Especially after all you've done for me," said Gabriel.

"I know you do, Gabriel," said Malinda, smiling, "but you have a calling that's more important than just being a farm boy."

"There's nothing wrong with just being a farm boy," he said firmly. "I would be honored to stay here and help your father."

"Oh, you might be happy for a while, but then you would wonder why you didn't go to Boston. I can see that in your eyes."

"What do you mean you can see in my eyes? There's not much there other than a little bit of blue," responded Gabriel smartly.

"Don't you know, the eyes are the mirror to a person's soul?" said Malinda.

"And what exactly do my eyes tell you?" questioned Gabriel in disbelief.

"They don't speak in words, but I can tell they're full of ambition and strength. And I know you've walked all this way by yourself from New York. You have a vision for your life that's more than this simple farm can offer."

Gabriel didn't have an answer for Malinda, partly because she was right. Something inside him told him his path in life was not to be a farm boy. He didn't know what exactly that path was, but he knew his job was to find it. He and Malinda walked along in silence, strolling by the small pond that sat close to the barn.

Malinda finally broke the silence as they walked. "Gabriel, I know you have your drum, but where are the drumsticks? I would love to hear you play before you leave."

"I don't have any drumsticks."

"Then how do you play?" asked Malinda.

All of a sudden, Gabriel felt small and embarrassed. He looked at Malinda and confessed. "Actually, I don't know how to play . . . yet! But I will learn."

"Well, what are you going to do? Mr. Arnold thinks you're a drummer boy. I imagine he's expecting you to play and keep beat while his militiamen march to Boston."

Gabriel stopped walking. "I don't know what I'm going to do. I found the drum in the river, and I thought it the only way I would be allowed to join the militia. But I've never played a drum in my life. I don't have any sticks, and I don't have anyone to teach me." He stopped. He knew he was getting carried away. "I'm sorry," he said. "It's just I really don't know what I'm going to do."

He slouched and looked down at his feet.

Malinda looked at him, turned her head slowly to the pond, and then smiled and exclaimed, "I know!" She took off, running to the bank of the pond where tall reeds stood in shallow water. The next thing Gabriel knew, Malinda was wading into the water.

"What are you doing?" he asked, chasing after her. "Are you looking for frogs, or what?"

Malinda didn't respond. As Gabriel reached the bank, she was working on pulling out a couple of the sturdy river cane reeds. These were the same kind of reeds often used as arrow shafts. She finally pulled two reeds from the water, their muddy roots still dripping. "Come on," she said.

Next thing Gabriel knew, Malinda was sprinting back toward the house. By the time he caught up with her, she had her father's axe in her hand. She laid one of the reeds down on a piece of wood and let the axe fall, cutting the reed off smoothly so it was about a foot long. She did the same to the other reed and then handed the pair to Gabriel. He stood there, looking puzzled at the reeds.

"Drumsticks," Malinda said brightly. "Hurry up and go get your drum."

Gabriel went inside, picked up his drum, and brought it back out into the warm sunshine. He put the sling for the drum around his neck and then slowly set one of the reeds down onto the surface of the drum. It gave a quick clean *pum* sound. "Hit it harder," said Malinda. "Haven't you ever seen someone beat a drum?"

He hit the drum harder, trying to create a rolling *rum-pum-pum* sound, but it just sounded like a bunch of racket. *Constance might as well be beating pots and pans in the kitchen with a wooden spoon*, he thought.

"Try it again," said Malinda. "Things like this take practice."

Gabriel tried, but he couldn't get it right. He could barely keep a simple beat on the drum. His frustration grew.

"Well, no matter," Malinda said with a smile. "You'll get it figured out. At least you have a pair of drumsticks now."

Gabriel smiled back, but he wasn't too sure having a pair of drumsticks was a good thing, after all. Captain Arnold and his militia would likely be leaving for Boston tomorrow, and the man might ask him to play. The thought filled him with both joy and fear. Any man marching along to the beat of his drum would have to drop his gun and cover his ears. And who could know what kind of effect his clambering rhythm would have on the horses? They may rear up and buck off their riders.

Benedict Arnold would quickly conclude he was no drummer boy. Gabriel would have no excuse other than to claim his sickness had somehow affected his playing ability. For all Gabriel knew, that may be true.

Hopefully Captain Arnold's militia already has a drummer boy, thought Gabriel. *One who can teach me how to play.*

"I'd better get back inside and help Constance with supper, and you'd better go back in and lay down a bit," said Malinda, starting up toward the house. "You need to look as fit as you can if Mr. Arnold is going to take you with him to Boston tomorrow."

Just the thought of marching along with Captain Arnold's men on the way to Boston filled his heart with joy, and for the moment, he forgot he didn't know how to play the drum. He stuffed the drumsticks in his back pocket, and before Malinda could turn to run up to the house, he caught her by the arm.

"Thank you," he said. "I needed those drumsticks, and you were clever enough to find a way to make them." He looked at Malinda's eyes and remembered what she had told him about the eyes being the mirror to the soul. He realized then he'd heard that saying before. He suddenly wanted to know where Malinda had heard it. "Where did you get that bit about the eyes being the mirror to the soul?"

"My mother read it to me from a book. I can't remember the name of it, but it's something I've always remembered, because it's true."

Gabriel looked away as a memory of his own mother suddenly overwhelmed him, "The eyes are the mirror to the soul . . . *Les yeux sont le miroir de l'âme.*"

"What did you say?" asked Malinda.

"My mother was French. She spoke to me in French and taught me to read and write in French, too. I knew I had heard that saying before, but I didn't remember until you told me about your mother reading to you. My mother told it to me a long time ago. So long I had almost forgotten. Thank you for reminding me."

"I love those kind of memories of my mother, too," said Malinda. She hugged Gabriel. "Don't ever forget them."

Gabriel and Malinda both turned to head back into the house. Mr. Fleming came in shortly afterward and made Gabriel lie down in bed. He did as he was told, even though he felt like running into town to show Benedict Arnold he was well. He felt like it was Christmas Eve! He was so excited about the next day, he could hardly get to sleep. Finally he managed to drift off by thinking of the march. One last night in the comfort of the Fleming home.

Gabriel awoke the next morning to the smell of frying bacon filling the Fleming farmhouse. He pulled the quilt back, stepped out of bed, and quickly got dressed. He wanted to leave no doubt in the mind of Captain Arnold he was fit enough to march to Boston. He would be dressed and ready to go by the time Arnold arrived.

Gabriel walked into the small kitchen where Malinda and Constance were cooking over the fire in the fireplace. Bacon was in one cast iron skillet, and some pancakes were cooking in another. Spotting a glass jar of maple syrup on the table, he knew he was in for a treat.

Mr. Fleming said, "Sit down, Gabriel. We wanted to send you off with a proper breakfast. We don't want you being hungry on the march, right, girls?"

Malinda and Constance turned and smiled. "It'll be ready in just a minute."

Even though Gabriel had been told to sit down, he helped pass out the plates and poured everyone a glass of milk, which must have just come from the Fleming cow, because it was still warm. Then Gabriel sat as Malinda and Constance brought over the food from the fire.

"Help yourself to the maple syrup. There's plenty where that came from," said Mr. Fleming. "The girls and I have some thirty maple trees tapped on the farm, and we had a good spring for collecting the sap. The weather was just warm enough to get the sap running."

Gabriel poured the syrup over the golden brown cakes on his plate and took a bite, when a knock rang out on the Flemings' door. His heart jumped with excitement. The knock had to be from Captain Arnold.

He stood up with his back straight and his chin high, ready to show Arnold he had returned to full health. Mr. Fleming went to the door and opened it. The man at the door was not Benedict Arnold.

"Good morning, John, won't you come in and have a bite to eat? The girls have cooked a wonderful breakfast," said Mr. Fleming in a welcoming voice.

"No, no, can't. Got too much to do at the post office in town. You know the mail's picked up something fierce since all those militiamen left to surround Boston. Some of 'em must send a letter a day back to loved ones," replied the man, still standing at the door. "Got this special note, supposed to be delivered to the young chap you got staying here with you. Good of Mr. Arnold to deliver that life-saving medicine on such a horribly stormy day. Arnold's a man this town is going to greatly miss while he's away heading up the militia in Boston town. Now, no time to spare. Gotta get back to town before the morning satchel of mail gets in. Have a good day."

And with that, the rambling man turned and left. Mr. Fleming stood at the door waving, a white piece of folded paper flapping in his hand.

Mr. Fleming turned back to the table, looked at the paper, and handed it to Gabriel. "It doesn't say who it's from. I wonder who could be sending you a letter here."

Gabriel was wondering the same, himself. He held the paper lightly between his fingers, unsure whether he actually wanted to open it. What if somehow the Lorings had found out where he had gone and were now urging him to return to New York? What if it was from Herbert Loring, the only person in the Loring household Gabriel liked? Maybe the letter was from Ben Daniels, the farmer he met at King's Bridge, with some type of warning.

"Don't just sit there, open it!" shouted Malinda from across the table.

Startled out of his daydream about whom the letter could be from, Gabriel slid his finger under the wax seal and slowly lifted the folded flap of paper. He gently unfolded the paper and flattened it onto the table. "Well, go on, read it!" exclaimed Malinda.

Gabriel cleared his throat and began to read aloud.

Dear Gabriel Cooper,

Late yesterday I received word from the militia commanders surrounding Boston that my services were urgently needed on a secret mission of great importance. It was requested I gather my Connecticut militiamen as soon as possible and begin the march. This will be a rugged march over difficult terrain and will ultimately conclude in a very dangerous undertaking. The march is much more difficult than traveling the road to Boston, and so it is with deepest regrets that I must inform you that you will not be able to accompany my militiamen and me on this journey. This is so, given the uncertain state of your health. We cannot be slowed down for any reason.

By the time you are reading this letter, my men and I will have already set out. The life of a true soldier, such as I, is full of perils. It is not for the weak, such as yourself. Return to New York or stay with the Flemings. They are a good, God-fearing family who I know would treat you well. I must now close, as time is now short and the night is already growing old. My glorious calling to victory awaits.

Your servant,
Colonel Benedict Arnold

Gabriel set the letter down on the table. He could not face Malinda, Constance, or Mr. Fleming. He didn't want them to tell him they were sorry or ask him what he was going to do now. He wanted to be alone, so he got up from the table without saying a word, opened the door, and ran out into the gathering morning light. He walked past the barn and down to the pond where Malinda had plucked the reeds for drumsticks the day before. He sat next to the bank. A few tree frogs were still chirping, not yet realizing the morning sun had risen. As he sat there, he began to wonder why he ever left New York. Doubts filled his mind, then anger. Why had Benedict Arnold not taken him along? Why would he tell Gabriel to go back to New York? Didn't he realize Gabriel knew that, by joining the militia, there was a chance he would face battle and possible death?

After the surge of anger, the doubts returned. He liked the Flemings. He could be happy here. What business did a boy have going off to fight, anyway? And that drum—he didn't even know how to play the thing. Even if he made it to Boston, the militiamen there would probably laugh at him after they heard him try to play. They would laugh until he felt like crying and running away, and then where would he go?

Gabriel felt a gentle hand on his shoulder. Malinda sat down next to him. "You've been out here by yourself for quite a while," she said. "I thought I would come find you, just to make sure you are all right."

"Well, I'm not all right," he said. "I'm angry and confused and . . . and . . ."

"You're not going to listen to what Mr. Arnold put in that letter, are you?" replied Malinda.

"What do you mean?" asked Gabriel.

"You are not about to go back to New York or stay here with us on the farm. Don't let Mr. Arnold confuse you."

"And why shouldn't I let him confuse me? It's not like I really know what I'm doing here in the first place."

"Don't say that, Gabriel. You do know what you're doing here. I'll tell you why you shouldn't listen to Mr. Arnold. He looks after one person in this life, and that's himself. Oh, he may have moments of what appear to be compassion—for example, bringing over that quinine when you had such a high fever—but he only does that to look important in the eyes of others. You noticed how the postmaster who brought the letter to you this morning knew right where to find you. He knew you had been sick and that Mr. Arnold had delivered the quinine to save your life. I guarantee Mr. Arnold made sure the whole town of New Haven knew what he had done to save a poor, helpless boy."

Gabriel interrupted, "Malinda, you shouldn't say such harsh things about Captain—I mean, Colonel—Arnold. He saved my life."

"I should say such harsh things, and I will," retorted Malinda. "I'm respectful of Mr. Arnold to his face only because I have to be. You just ask my father what happened between him and Mr. Arnold a few years ago. He will tell you of Benedict Arnold's selfish motives. The building in New Haven where Mr. Arnold has his drugstore . . . well, it should have belonged to my father."

"What are you talking about?" asked Gabriel

"Father knew how difficult farming could be and was looking to open up a store that sold farm equipment and seed, so he could stop working full-time in the fields. Farming was exceptionally hard for Father, since he had no sons to help him. He asked around town if any buildings may be coming up for sale. A man named Mr. Tanner told Father he would sell a building he owned along Main Street. Father was surprised by the quick response and even more surprised by the low price Mr. Tanner was asking for the building. Mr. Tanner said he would sell it to Father only if he had all of the money in hand. Father said he would get the money but asked that Mr. Tanner not tell anyone else about the building being for sale. Father went and sold some of his best farmland to raise the rest of the money needed. It only took him a couple of weeks before he had it all. He was so excited."

Gabriel looked confused, "What does this have to do with Colonel Arnold?"

"I am getting to that part, just be patient," responded Malinda. "Two days before he took his money to Mr. Tanner, Father spoke with Benedict Arnold, who had stopped by to deliver some medicine for Mother. He told Mr. Arnold about his plans to open up a farm store and said Mr. Tanner was asking a very fair price for the building. Benedict promised Father he wouldn't tell anyone about his plans since the deal wasn't completed yet. Father took the money from his lockbox the next day and went to hand it all to Mr. Tanner. Mr. Tanner told him he was sorry, but the building was already sold. He said Benedict Arnold had come by earlier that morning and offered Mr. Tanner more money than he was asking for the building and threw in a lifetime supply of whatever medicines he may need. Mr. Tanner swore he hadn't told anyone about the building being for sale, but he couldn't refuse Mr. Arnold's offer. Mr. Arnold, that selfish brute, bought the building right out from under Father. He opened up his drugstore in the building and never told anyone what he did to Father."

"That's horrible. Why was your father so nice to Colonel Arnold when he came by the house?" asked Gabriel.

"Father says it was just business and that it was his own stupid fault for flapping his jaw about buying the building from Mr. Tanner for a fair price. Mind you, he's certainly not Mr. Arnold's best friend. Did you notice he didn't jump at the chance to have Mr. Arnold stay for dinner the other night? Still, even if Father had felt harshly toward Mr. Arnold, he would have forgiven him by now. Father has told me more than once the Bible tells us to forgive seventy times seven. He usually tells me that when Constance has done something mean, like breaking one of my doll's arms off."

"Was your father able to buy back his farmland?" questioned Gabriel.

"No, and no other buildings have come up for sale that Father could afford. We grow just enough food for ourselves, and Father hires himself out to work at other people's farms or at the sawmill." She looked at Gabriel squarely. "Do you see now why I tell you not to listen to Benedict Arnold?"

Gabriel nodded his head. He truly felt sorry for Malinda and her family. The thought of marching with Colonel Arnold now seemed repulsive.

"I'm sorry about what happened to your father, Malinda," he said, "but I still don't know how I'm supposed to get to Boston now that I've been left behind."

"Nothing has changed about how you are going to get to Boston, Gabriel," Malinda said softly. "You left New York knowing how you would get there. You would walk. That hasn't changed. The fleeting hope you could join up with Mr. Arnold's militiamen before you reached Boston doesn't change anything."

He knew this was true. "You sure must want me to leave, because you're doing a good job persuading me I should continue on my journey to Boston."

"I don't want you to leave, Gabriel. I've only known you for a short time, but you are already a dear friend, and I want you to stay a close friend to me even if you are going to be off fighting in Boston."

"I will stay a close friend to you no matter where I am."

"Then you will go on?" asked Malinda.

"Yes, I will go."

Malinda took Gabriel's hand. "And I will pray for your safe return."

★10★

A GIFT

Gabriel headed back up to the house with Malinda. Mr. Fleming was already out splitting wood. He put down his axe and wiped his forehead with his shirtsleeve as they approached.

"Constance, could you go fetch me a pail of water, please?" asked Mr. Fleming.

Sweat dripped down from Mr. Fleming's face as the tall, lanky man sat down on a stump and let out a sigh. "Gabriel, life is full of people who let you down and circumstances that turn out to disappoint you. I've had a few of both in my life, but there's one thing you have to remember . . . be true to yourself. Don't let others discourage you from taking the path chosen for your life. You are the only one who can know that path. Find it, and then hold on to it with all of your heart."

"Yes, sir," responded Gabriel, "but the hard part is figuring out what path you are supposed to be on."

Mr. Fleming chuckled, stood up, and picked up his axe to resume his chopping. He said in a ringing tone, "'And this above all, to thine own self be true, and it must follow as the night the day, thou can'st not then be false to any man.'"

Gabriel looked with surprise at Mr. Fleming. "I've heard that before."

"You'll find Shakespeare's play *Hamlet* on my bookshelf inside the house, along with other plays and poems he's written."

Gabriel nodded. "*Hamlet.* I knew I had heard that quote before. My mother and father took me to see it when I was little. I mostly remember being scared of the ghost. I have been frightened by the thought of spirits ever since."

"Shakespeare did like to frighten his audience on occasion." Mr. Fleming laughed. "But he always seemed to wind a great many truths into his tales. I hope what I told you makes sense, Gabriel. You may take all the time you need to reach a decision about whether you will return to New York, stay here, or travel on. I only ask that your choice be definite and that, once you've decided, you'll not waiver."

"I've already decided I'll continue on to Boston, sir," replied Gabriel.

Mr. Fleming took a step toward Gabriel, patted him on the back, and then grabbed his shoulders, giving a firm squeeze. "Well done, Gabriel. Don't lose heart. When will you depart?"

"I'm afraid if I stay too long, I'll be tempted to change my mind. I'll head out in the morning," said Gabriel. As soon as the words had left his mouth, he wished he could take them back. Somehow, saying them aloud to Mr. Fleming suddenly made leaving real.

"Very good, son. That will give us time to prepare another farewell meal and pack up some food to take with you," said Mr. Fleming with a broad smile.

Mr. Fleming was true to his word. He left that afternoon and returned with three plump quail. The hunting was still good in the hills near New Haven, and he was obviously a good shot. Gabriel wished he could stay and have Mr. Fleming teach him how to shoot, but he already said he was leaving. In the morning, he would be gone.

He tried to shake this thought from his mind by helping Mr. Fleming pluck the quails' feathers and then mount them on a spit. Malinda and Constance took turns turning the spit gently over the fire in the hearth. The succulent juices from the birds dripped slowly onto the flames, and a wonderful smell filled the small cabin. Malinda and Constance made cornbread and tea to go with the quail.

The meal was quite possibly the best one Gabriel could remember. The quail was the juiciest and most tender meat he'd ever eaten. And just when he thought it couldn't get any better, Malinda left the table to return with an apple cobbler she'd made.

"I was just getting ready to say the only thing this meal was missing is dessert, but I'd have spoken too soon," said

Mr. Fleming, now sniffing the sweet aroma filling the air. "That, Malinda dear, looks delicious, and I suggest we not delay in finding out exactly how delicious it really is."

Malinda set the dessert down on the table and dished up a steaming portion for everyone. Gabriel ate the dessert, savoring every bite, remembering how hungry he'd been earlier in his journey. Then, as the last bits of apple cobbler were dished out, Mr. Fleming left the table for a moment and returned holding something behind his back. "Gabriel, in addition to this fine meal and the food we have already packed for you, I have something else."

"Make him guess, Papa!" shouted Constance.

"Guess? Oh yes, very well," responded Mr. Fleming. "Gabriel, what do you think is hidden behind my back?"

Gabriel had no idea what was hidden behind Mr. Fleming's back and had to think for a few moments before he cried out, "A new knife?"

"No, guess again," said Mr. Fleming.

"A hatchet."

"No again, but it is somewhat of a cross between a tool and a weapon."

Constance was beaming with glee with the progression of the guessing game. She always loved to make people guess, sometimes over the silliest things.

A cross between a tool and a weapon, thought Gabriel. "A trap for catching animals," shouted Gabriel.

"I'll consider that close enough." Mr. Fleming held out a fishing hook and some fishing line.

Gabriel took the hook and line from him. "Thank you. I'm sure to catch some big fish with this."

"There are plenty of streams and ponds on the road that runs north of here to Hartford and on into Massachusetts. You should find the fishing good—at least good enough to keep you from going hungry," said Mr. Fleming. "Now then, why don't we all enjoy a little music before we turn in."

Mr. Fleming went to his bedroom and returned with a fiddle and bow. Gabriel sat back in the large rocking chair in front of the fire and listened to the songs flowing from the fiddle. He recognized some of the songs, such as "Yankee Doodle," but he'd never heard many of them. Malinda and Constance rose to dance, when Mr. Fleming began to play a minuet. They motioned for Gabriel to get up and join them, but he just shook his head.

"Come now," said Malinda. "We'll teach you if you don't know how."

After finally being pulled from his chair by Malinda and Constance, Gabriel found himself trying to mimic a courteous bow and then several steps to the right and several steps to the left. In the process of trying to watch Malinda's feet instead of his own, his legs became tangled, and he toppled over, falling to the floor. Malinda and Constance laughed and pulled him back to his feet. His face turned two shades of red, but he tried to follow the steps again. None too soon, the song ended, and Gabriel quickly plopped back down into the rocking chair.

"What elegant dancers you all are," said Mr. Fleming, clapping his hands. Then he picked up his fiddle once more. "One last song, and then it's off to bed." Notes began to pour from the fiddle, entrancing Gabriel with a mournfully sweet song. Mr. Fleming sang no words, yet the notes seemed to speak to Gabriel all the same. The melody went on softly until he found himself being gently shaken by Malinda. "Gabriel, Gabriel, you fell asleep. It's time for bed."

"Oh, yes, I must have just dozed off." Gabriel rose slowly from the chair and half-walked, half-stumbled to the bed. He crawled in and quickly fell asleep. As he did, he thought to himself how hard it would be to leave this place come morning.

★ 11 ★
LEAVING

It was time to leave, and Gabriel knew it. Standing just outside the door to the cabin, the morning sun shone brightly. He had eaten a filling breakfast, but there hadn't been much conversation at the breakfast table. In a way, he was glad, hoping it would somehow make it easier to leave the Fleming farm.

"Now then," said Malinda, handing him his sack, "I sewed up the tear in your blanket, folded it up as a pack, and filled it with dried beef, biscuits, and a few bits of maple sugar I've been saving. Father found an old canteen that I filled with some tea. All of your belongings are in there, including a beautiful ring and a piece of paper. I'm not sure what the piece of paper is, but I saw it had writing on it."

"That is a note from my mother," replied Gabriel.

"Don't worry, I didn't read it," said Malinda.

"It would have been all right if you had. Maybe you would know what its meaning is more than I do. At least I know you understand why I keep it."

"Yes, I do understand, Gabriel," said Malinda, handing over the pack. "Don't forget your drum and these fine drumsticks we made."

"I can't forget that," he said. He picked up his drum and stuffed the sticks down into his pack. He took his special ring out and stuck it into his pocket where he always kept it, and then tied up the sack, slinging it over his back.

Gabriel stood in the sunlight that filtered softly down in front of the cabin. He looked at Malinda, Constance, and Mr. Fleming and was unable to move.

He felt a wet streak begin to move slowly down his cheek. Next thing he knew, he had thrown off his pack and drum and run to Malinda and Constance, giving each of them a hug. Next came Mr. Fleming, who grabbed him with his strong arms and gave him such a tight hug he thought he might suffocate.

Wiping the tears from his eyes, Gabriel stammered, "You'll write, won't you? I'm not sure exactly where I'll be, but I've been told to find a Nathaniel Greene when I get to Boston. I think he's in charge of the Rhode Island militia. I want to know all that is going on around the farm, just as if I were here."

"We will write you often, don't worry, Gabriel," said Malinda.

Gabriel picked up his pack and drum again. He stood looking at the three people who saved his life, nursed him back to health, and helped him remember what it was like to have a real family again. He struggled to move his feet. At this moment, every inch of him felt like staying. Still, he began to turn away from them.

Concentrating on putting one foot in front of the other, he was some distance away when he decided to look back. Down by the small house, he saw the three of them still standing there, waving. He fought back tears and walked on back to the road that would take him to Boston.

Gabriel tried to distance himself from Malinda and the Fleming farm as quickly as he could, for fear he would go running back. Leaving her was even harder than he imagined. Yet he remembered her words to him: *I want you to stay a close friend to me even if you are going to be off fighting in Boston.*

He felt a sense of pride. Now he had something to fight for and return to.

He held his head higher and began to march his pace. He soon found his way back to the Boston Post Road and arrived in the town of New Haven shortly after. He walked down the street as the town was beginning to bustle with activity. As he walked past Benedict Arnold's drugstore, he wondered where Arnold and his men were at that moment, still feeling betrayed about being left behind.

When he reached the edge of town, he saw a stone marker: "Hartford 39 miles." Feeling strong and refreshed, he told himself he could reach Hartford in two days. He had the provisions from the Flemings to eat along the way, and the weather was good.

But just beyond New Haven's West Rock, he needed to rest. The fever, he thought, had taken its toll on his stamina. Perhaps reaching Hartford would take longer than two days. He would have to temper his pace.

During one of his breaks along the side of the road, Gabriel's thoughts turned to the warships he had seen atop the hill, and he couldn't help but feel a sense of urgency to reach Boston. The battle for Boston would be over by the time he got there, and then what? He was doing the best he could. He had to keep up his strength. Finding the Flemings had been by providence alone. He couldn't take the chance of falling ill again. Whatever the circumstance, Ben Daniels had told him to find and report to Nathaniel Greene. That was his duty.

Fortunately, as the days passed, there was very little traffic on the road. Still, there were many loyalists along the route who would not be sympathetic to his journey. He had discovered that firsthand in his meetings with Bradford Grimm. The possibility of receiving a good thrashing, or worse yet, being strung up from a tree, was very real if a loyalist got a hold of him. He also knew other orphaned boys had been forced to join His Majesty's troops.

Despite the risks, he was more determined than ever to reach the militia. He had come such a long way. Neither the

Lorings, nor loyalists, nor illness had stopped him. It was on to Boston to serve his country.

Malinda had packed a good amount of food for his journey. After the end of each long day of walking, Gabriel would sit down and eat a bite. Lying down to sleep when the stars came out, he would be back up and ready to move with the rising of the sun.

Almost a week had passed since he left the Flemings' farm. He still had some dried meats, hardtack, and whortle-berries left in his pack. Every time he sat down to have a bite to eat and a drink from his canteen, he thought of Malinda and the rest of her family. The food brought back fond memories of the Flemings, which comforted him on his lonely journey.

He reached the town of Hartford almost six full days after he left the Flemings. His food supply was running a little low. As he passed through town, he would keep an eye out for any food he might collect as he journeyed on, but he would not stop. Over the past two days, he'd been able to walk for over three hours before needing a rest, and he seemed to cover more ground. He walked through the side streets of the town, avoiding the busy shops that lined the main thorough-fare, and quickly reached the north side of town.

It was afternoon now, and Gabriel stood in front of a stone marker along the side of the road that read, "Springfield 32 Miles."

"Massachusetts," he whispered to himself. He had chosen the northernmost branch of the Post Road, since it was the shortest path to Massachusetts. He may still be many miles from Boston, but at least he would soon be standing on Massachusetts soil. This was a colony filled with patriots, ready and willing to fight, and he was almost there. Excited by the thought of being one step closer to Massachusetts, he pressed on with a new vigor. He walked briskly, and soon, Hartford was out of sight.

Gabriel entered a wooded area where the road wound around huge oak trees. The sun was lowering itself into the western sky, and he could hear the chorus of chirping tree frogs beginning to fill the air. He listened closely and heard the low barking sound of a bullfrog. Then he heard another and another low, gravelly croak. The scratchy sound of the deep-throated bullfrogs gave him an idea. Where there were bullfrogs, there was bound to be a pond, and where there was a pond, there were bound to be fish. He could picture a pond just off the road, with flies and bugs skimming the water and huge fish jumping out to eat them, splashing back into the pond and sending ripples through the water.

Gabriel left the road, being careful to remember which way he was heading. He followed the sound of the frogs, and he soon found a clearing with a nice-sized pond lined with reeds and bulrush. "This will do nicely," he said to himself. He rolled up his pants to his knees and waded out to pluck a strong reed from the muddy ground. He then waded back over to solid ground and cut the narrow end of the reed off with his knife. He took the fine point of his knife and put a small hole through the end of the reed. Unrolling his pack, he took out his fishing line and carefully threaded it through the hole in the reed, tying a hook at the end of the gut. He took a nearby rock and began to pry up some of the soft dirt along the side of the pond. Before long, he had several huge, wriggling worms, one of which he threaded onto his hook.

Armed with his newly formed fishing pole in hand, Gabriel stepped back out through the reeds and stood where the water was about knee-deep. Holding the line and hook gathered up in his hand, he threw it out away from the reeds. It plunked into the water, and he stood silently, waiting for his line to move.

The pond was just as Gabriel had imagined. The hot sun sinking in the sky seemed to signal the fish to begin their feeding frenzy on all sorts of bugs that flitted over the pond. He saw fish after fish jump and splash, but not one seemed to be interested in his line. "Patience . . . patience," he muttered to himself. The sun was sinking fast, and he knew he was running out of time. He slowly pulled his line out of the water to cast it once again to his farthest reach.

No sooner had he thrown his line back than something grabbed his hook and gave a mighty tug. The reed began to slip out of Gabriel's hand. He quickly grabbed it with his other hand and gave a jerk to set the hook. His catch began struggling even more. He wrapped the line around the end of his pole to reel in a large fish. He struggled with his prey but, finally, a large green and silver fish lay flopping at his feet.

He stuck the end of his pole down into the soft mud below the water and, with both hands, reached down to pick up the fish. Its cold and slimy scales tried to wriggle free. As he picked it up, he tried to guess its weight. It had to be close to ten pounds and looked to be some type of bass.

He wished he could show off his catch to someone, but he was alone. Nevertheless, he held his fish up high as if to show the world what fine work his fishing line and hook had accomplished. It seemed to Gabriel that the chorus of chirping and croaking frogs grew a bit louder, as if to say, "Well done, *ribbit . . . croak*, congratulations."

He looked around the pond as the last sliver of sun sank below the sky and said with a loud and official voice, "Thank you, thank you all."

He lowered the fish back down between his knees and pulled the hook from its mouth. Wrapping his line and hook around his pole, he waded back through the reeds to the bank of the pond. He found a flat rock not far from shore, set his catch down, and went to collect some firewood.

He gathered some paper-thin bark from a nearby birch tree and nestled it down into a bundle of twigs. Pulling the flint rock from his bag, he laid it next to the birch bark and struck the flat edge of his knife on the flint. Immediately, a gush of red sparks sprung from the flint onto the bark. They smoldered, but the wood did not catch fire. He struck his knife again, and this time, as soon as the sparks landed on the bark, he leaned down and gave a gentle blow. The sparks began to glow and smoke, and then the bark burst into flames. Gabriel continued blowing slowly and evenly, carefully applying the twigs onto the growing flames. After he had a good flame going with the twigs, he started adding larger pieces of wood he had gathered. Soon he had a blazing fire.

He sat there for a moment and marveled at his fire. He had seen his father start a fire in the hearth in his old home in New York a hundred times. He himself had even started many, but this fire was different. It was all his own, and its warmth would cook the fish he had caught. A sense of pride like he'd never felt before welled up inside him. He gave a whoop of excitement and sprang up to prepare his fish.

He cut off the fish's head and tail and gutted it. Then he took a sturdy stick and whittled down the end to make a point that he stuck through the fish. Taking the stick over to the fire, he carefully held the fish over the flames. The fish sizzled over the open flames and soon succulent juice began dripping over the fire. The smell of the cooking meat made Gabriel's mouth water. This was going to be a feast.

He did not leave the fish on the flames too long, partly because he did not want to overcook it and partly because he was so hungry. The scales had begun to crinkle and turn black from the heat, so he removed the fish from the fire and carefully rested it on the flat rock. He took out his knife and cut open the fish. The flaky, juicy meat fell off the bones. He grabbed the pieces and began stuffing them into his mouth. The fish tasted so good, he decided to try to slow down so he could enjoy it longer. He wasn't sure when he'd be able to enjoy such a delicacy again. He spoke a silent thank-you to Mr. Fleming for giving him the fishing line and hook.

The night had completely overtaken the pond now, and Gabriel sat by the fire, finishing off the last morsels of fish. Hot coals glowed red and white in the fire. The flames danced, sending sparks drifting up into the clear night sky. He lay on his back and watched the sparks, trying to see how high they would go before disappearing into the blackness. They always vanished, leaving nothing but the stars glittering in the sky.

Gabriel often wondered about the stars. Why had God put them in the sky? How far away were they? What made them shine? What made them twinkle? He had read some science books in his father's shop, but nothing about stars.

"You can learn from these." His father's voice rang in his mind. He missed his father . . . and then his mother . . . and then Malinda. With these thoughts of stars drifting through his head, he fell asleep, the frogs now chirping a song of peace and contentment.

★ 12 ★

THE BATTLE BEGINS

Over the next several days Gabriel covered many miles. His strength and resolve were renewed.

Having left New York in April, it was mid–June when he crossed the river into Springfield. He strolled into town in the late afternoon. The town's main street was abuzz with activity. It seemed a bit unusual to him. *Why would the town be so busy at this hour?* he wondered.

Several men rode in on their horses and dismounted. The townsfolk swarmed around them, so Gabriel walked closer to see what the commotion was about. With so many people crowded tightly together, he couldn't hear what the men were saying. He turned and walked away toward a modest wooden building with a sign out front that said, "Tavern." When he turned back once more, he saw the riders mount their saddles and gallop off. He peered into the crowd, still trying to figure out what was going on, but he was too far away.

He walked over to the storefront of the tavern and went inside. The room was empty except for a stout, round man standing behind the bar. Gabriel set his things down in a corner and walked over to the man standing at a large wooden table. "I'd like something to eat, sir, and I have coin," he said.

"Sure, anything you like, young man. I've got a fine piece of venison on the fire, and I'll throw in a drink for free. I'm just glad to have someone here to talk with about the news in Boston. All the town has been clamoring for news and talking at the post office. I haven't had but a handful of customers all day. Charlie's my name. What's yours?" asked the round-faced man.

"I am Gabriel. What news?"

"What news? Where have you been, lad? Why, the whole town is talking about it."

"No, I haven't heard, I . . . I've been away. What news?" Gabriel asked. Thoughts were flashing through his mind of the warships he had seen. Had they reached Boston? Had they blasted their cannons at the militia?

"Well, a couple of nights ago," Charlie began, "the men of the village militias moved out onto Charlestown Peninsula, just a stone's throw from the city of Boston itself. They dug trenches and made walls of dirt, all in the middle of the night. With the rising sun, the king's troops saw what the militias had done but, by then, they were already dug in. Some Royal Navy ships spotted them, and they tried blasting their cannon at the men, but the militia had dug their trenches on top of a hill. Breed's Hill is what they call it. The Navy couldn't get their cannon raised up high enough from the ships to reach the top of the hill. I guess they blasted away most of the morning, but they didn't harm a hair on a single militiaman."

"How do you know all this?" interrupted Gabriel in disbelief.

"I know it 'cause I heard it from Zachariah Smith. He's a farmer just east of here, and he heard it directly from a soldier on horseback sent to round up any surrounding militia."

"What then? Tell me more. What then of the patriots?"

Charlie continued, "Well them lobsterbacks just couldn't stand having our farmers and fishermen taking ground so close to Boston so, about mid-morning, the Navy started pounding the heights in Charlestown, and their flashy officers started to gather up a couple thousand more of their soldiers to take that hill. My guess is they figured they could just walk right up the hill, thinking they'd just scare the militiamen out of their trenches and send them running home."

Charlie stepped away from the table and walked toward the fire, where he removed a piece of venison for Gabriel. "I'm sorry," he said. "About forgot I was supposed to be feeding you." At the moment, though, Gabriel didn't care about a piece of venison. He was completely focused on finding out what happened on Breed's Hill. The round-faced man stepped away from the table again and reached up on a shelf to pull down a mug. "And I about forgot to give you that drink I promised." He reached down below the table, pulled up a bottle, and emptied it into the mug. Gabriel didn't know what it was, nor did he care.

"Please, sir . . . tell me more," Gabriel's voice was full of anticipation.

"The story! Ah, yes, the story. Don't worry now. Where was I?"

Gabriel responded impatiently. "The hill—you said the king's troops marched on Breed's Hill,"

"The hill, oh yes. The generals didn't think we'd fight. I guess they didn't learn anything from Lexington and Concord. Well, the militia boys had their muskets blastin' all afternoon, and Generals Howe and Clinton and all those fancy uniforms haven't been able to take the hill yet. Mind you now, this all happened yesterday, and not a word to say otherwise," said Charlie with a smile beaming across his face.

Gabriel should have been delighted by the news, but he was discouraged. He was missing out. He pictured himself on top of the hill with the other patriots, his drum in his hand, beating a rhythmic cadence to encourage the militias to hold off the soldiers marching up the hill. He had walked close to two hundred miles, and now his chance to fight could be gone. What if this would be the battle that sent the troops out of Boston and changed the way King George treated the colonies? Surely, thought Gabriel, things would change from here on out. He wondered if there would even be any other battles, or would this fight be it?

He looked down and began to eat the venison the tavern keeper had set before him.

"What's the matter," asked Charlie. "What's that frown on your face, lad? You aren't from one those loyalist families, are you?"

"No. No, I'm not. It's just that—"

He couldn't finish his sentence. The abrupt entrance of a man who came bustling over to Charlie interrupted him. He recognized the man from the crowd outside.

"Charlie, Charlie," he quickly shouted. "They ran out . . . it's over . . . had to fall back."

"Hold it, slow down, Paul," said Charlie, trying to calm the man. "Who ran out, and who fell back?"

"No . . . no, you don't understand," said Paul, still upset. "The militia ran out of ammunition. They had to fall back off of Breed's Hill . . . retreated to another hill. One of the militia messengers just rode into town to tell the news. Said they abandoned the peninsula to the lobsterbacks and fell back to save headquarters at Cambridge."

"God help us," muttered Charlie. "How many men were hurt?"

"Over a hundred. There's plenty of dead and wounded on both sides, though. Word is our provincials stood their ground as best they could. The regulars just marched right up against the redoubt twice and were repelled. On the third advance, they forced our boys back. The messenger said it was the bloodiest battle anyone's ever seen. I am off to Cambridge with the others. There's been a general call to arms!"

Gabriel was both thrilled and terrified, all at once. There may still be fighting. There may still be a place for him in the militia. But there may also be death and destruction. He had known this in the back of his mind all along, but now it was real. Despite these butterflies in his stomach, he knew he could overcome his fears. He had been doing just that ever since his parents died. With as much boldness as he could muster, he asked Paul, "If you are going to help in the fight, can I go with you?"

Paul smirked. "You got a gun?"

"No," replied Gabriel. "I have a drum, though."

"Where I'm going, we need men with guns, not boys with drums. Go back home to the farm, and tell your pa to get his gun. You can help by staying put and helping your ma with the chores."

This stranger could not have known how these words cut at Gabriel like a knife, but they did just that. They had cut deeply, and Gabriel was angry.

He was tired of being told to go back home, and he was tired of being reminded he didn't have a father or a mother.

He'd just walked over one hundred and forty miles, and this stranger wanted him to go home?

Without another thought, he let his anger fly. "I HAVE NO HOME! I HAVE NO FARM! I HAVE NO FATHER!

I WALKED ALL THE WAY FROM NEW YORK, AND I WILL MAKE IT TO BOSTON! I WILL FIGHT! I WILL . . . I WILL!"

A shocked expression appeared on both the barkeep's and the stranger's faces. Paul spoke first. "Easy, lad . . . easy. Nobody said you had to stay here. I'm sure they can find a place for a drummer boy, especially since they got some fancy general from Virginia coming up here to take over. Chances are he'll want some order to things, and every regiment will need a drummer boy."

"Then let me go with—" Gabriel started but was interrupted.

Charlie the barkeep held up a hand. "You mean to tell me they're gonna let some southerner take over the New England militias?" Now Charlie was the angry one, with his face reddened and wrinkled. "They're gonna replace Israel Putnam, good Old Put, as commander of our New England men? And what about Colonel Prescott and Major Warren? Why, Dr. Warren was among the best men at Lexington and Concord."

Paul shook his head, a look of remorse on his face. "They say Dr. Warren was killed in the battle—shot, bayoneted, and tossed in the ditch by those dirty redcoats. As for what this fellow from Virginia means to do, I'm not sure, but he'll have a hard time getting New Englanders to listen to him. That's for sure."

Charlie shook his head. "Not Dr. Warren. There's none braver or smarter. What a shame. And to think some Virginian is going to come up here and try to match the likes of men like Joseph Warren. It'll never happen."

Although Gabriel's temper had cooled, his determination to reach Boston had not. It might be good for him to know more about this Virginian. Maybe he could find a place for him in the militia. "Where is this general from Virginia now? Is he here in Springfield? What's his name?"

Paul answered. "His name is Washington . . . George Washington. I couldn't say for sure where he is at the moment but, last I heard, he was traveling by carriage up from New York. Should be in the main camp at Cambridge any day now."

"Then I am coming with you," said Gabriel firmly. "That's where you said you're headed, to Cambridge."

Paul gave a look of regret and sympathy, and Gabriel guessed what was coming. "I cannot take you with me. I am on a single horse packed with supplies. I do not have room for you and your drum. I'm sorry, but that is the way of things. Perhaps if you start out on the road, you will find another rider who has more room than I."

Gabriel expected nothing less. He remembered Malinda's words when Benedict Arnold had left him behind. *You left New York knowing how you would get to Boston. You would walk.* Nothing had changed for Gabriel. He would walk, and he would walk right now. He was tired of Charlie and Paul's chatter. He paid his bill, shoved the rest of the venison in his pack, and left Springfield, bound and determined to reach Cambridge before the fighting was over.

★ 13 ★
THE NOTE

Gabriel pushed his chair back, picked up his pack and drum, and stepped out into the street. He felt around in his pocket, and his fingers touched his ring and the change left over from his meal at the tavern at Springfield.

I have plenty of coppers left and two good legs. There's no reason why I can't make it to Boston in less than a week, he thought. He strode out of town as confident as ever. As he left the town, he saw a marker on the road. "Worcester, 52 Miles." Gabriel once again began his own patriotic pace, determined to join the cause.

The weather had been nearly perfect ever since the torrential rain earlier in his journey. Now it was getting warmer, almost hot. He took off his jerkin and wrapped it over his drum. The heat would not slow him down.

He stopped to fill his canteen every once in a while, and he still left the road whenever he heard approaching hoof beats. *Soon,* he thought, *I will be at the Cambridge encampment looking for Nathaniel Greene. I'm sure of it.*

The next few days passed quickly. As Gabriel passed by the towns on the Post Road, he saw other men on the road. Some were riding; some, like him, walked in small groups. Palmer, Brookfield, Leicester—farmers mostly. They carried old muskets, axes, swords, hatchets, and knives. The older men did not talk to him. They would stare and sometimes snicker. Some would chide or taunt him. "What'cha looking to do there, sonny, throw that beat-up old drum at the lobsterbacks?" one called out. Gabriel thought it best to just keep to himself.

The fishing had been good in the few streams and ponds he passed. There had certainly been enough to keep him fed, but he was growing tired of fish. Fishing slowed him down, too. He had to stop, find bait, catch a fish, gut it, build a fire, and then cook it. Keeping to himself, he would let his fire burn just long enough to cook the fish he caught. Then, with stars and moon overhead, he would throw his blanket down on the hard ground and try to find a spot comfortable enough for some sleep.

On the fourth day out of Springfield, just beyond Worcester, Gabriel reached a densely wooded area along the road. He stopped to marvel at the enormous trees that grew up along the path. As he stood looking up at a giant sycamore tree, he noticed the sound of water running nearby. Leaving the road, he began weaving his way through the giant tree trunks toward the sound, which was growing louder now.

Swatting his way through some underbrush, he finally came to a small river lined with the tall trees, whose branches reached over the water to touch the trees on the other side.

The water offered a refreshing break from the heat, so he set down his things, pulled off his socks and shoes, and waded in. He walked out to the middle, where the water reached his knees. Something piqued his interest on just the other side. He waded over to see several bushes hanging close to the river, covered in blue berries. "Whortleberries," exclaimed Gabriel. He had long since run out of the berries that Malinda had given him from her farm.

He hurriedly splashed back across the river, dumped out his belongings in his pack onto the sandy beach, and took the empty blanket back across the river with him. Soon, he had his blanket nearly overflowing with plump, juicy blue whortleberries.

He took the berries back to the beach, leaned back against a smooth rock, and started popping berries into his mouth one by one. The berries were perfectly sweet. The taste reminded him of the times his mother had baked him whortleberry pies, one of his favorites. He felt the warm sun filtering through the trees and leaned back, continuing to enjoy the berries. The sand was soft, much softer than the hard ground he'd grown used to sleeping on.

Gabriel looked at his belongings dumped into the sand. These few things—his note, knife, flint rock, drumsticks, canteen, fishing line and hook, coins, and the ring in his pocket—were all of his worldly possessions. It wasn't much, but it was enough. Of all these things, he picked up the one that was most precious to him, the note his mother had written him. She had written it shortly after she became ill. *She was always so optimistic*, thought Gabriel. *Even when she wrote the note, it was clear she truly believed she would get better.*

He read the note often, not just to bring back memories of his mother, but also because he could never quite figure out what it was that his mother was trying to say. He once thought his mother must have had the fever and wasn't thinking straight when she wrote it, but her handwriting was clear with not one waver of her pen.

His mother had always loved poetry, which accounted for the poetic style of the note, but as with other poems Gabriel had read, the meaning was foggy and seemed to change from one day to the next. Still, reading it always gave him a strange sense of hope.

So Gabriel laid his back down in the soft sand, held the note up to the glittering green canopy overhead, and read it once more.

To my darling son, Gabriel,

You are the light of my life, my joy, my peace, my gift from God. In you flows a river of strength that you as yet count to be a mere babbling brook. Just as I grew up watching the rushing waters of the

Seine, so too I will spend the rest of my days watching the river of strength grow in you. For it is to the heights of the Seine that you may wish to go one day.

The decision will be yours, my son, whether you will enter the house on the heights that changes stone to silver, rocks to rubies, and water to wine. To pass through that door, there is a price, and one only you can pay. The price was too high for me, and so I find myself here—a sacrifice I have not made, for the joy of my life is priceless. Look at what surrounds me. What more could I want? I pray you may know the same, but soon the choice will be yours, and whatever it may be, my love for you will follow. Gabriel, I have so much to tell you as the seasons turn, but for now, let me tell you this: I love you more than life itself.

Your most loving mother

Gabriel folded the note back up in its wax paper cover and stuck it into his pocket. It did not make any more sense to him now than it had the hundreds of other times he had read it. He knew the Seine was in France, but then there was the "decision" Gabriel's mother had said he must make about entering a house. That made no sense to him at all. What decision would there be about whether or not to enter a house? Either you walk through the door, or you don't. What difference would it make? Was this some magical house that could somehow change you once you entered the door?

Still, there was one thing perfectly clear about the note: his mother had loved him dearly. This thought saddened Gabriel. His mother was not able to tell him more as she had promised, because her illness worsened the day after she wrote the note. Her fever intensified, and she died only a few days later. Why hadn't she told him more? He wished she were still alive and could explain these things to him. But he had wished that thousands of times, and it never came true.

He was tired now. The sand was so soft, he thought of just spending the night here and having a nice fire. It wouldn't be too long before it was dark, and the thought of venturing on to only find another restless night on hard ground sealed the decision in his mind. He would stay put.

Gabriel gathered some wood and, using his knife and flint rock, soon started a fire. He stuck his knife in the sand and leaned back, watching the growing darkness reveal the heavenly dusting of stars that began to fill the sky. Looking off to the northwest, he could see tall, puffy clouds on the horizon. The bright white contours of the clouds were accentuated by the blackening sky. As he watched the clouds, they seemed to grow before his eyes, their tops ascending like a boiling froth of water. The sun continued to sink, causing the clouds to turn shades of pink and purple. Watching the amazing display of colors, Gabriel saw a flash of lightning bounce around in the tops of the clouds. The flash of lightning confirmed what these clouds were: thunderheads.

Well, he thought, *I may get wet tonight, but at least I'll have a soft bed here in the sand.*

Gabriel always liked thunderstorms. He found their awesome display of power through lightning and wind fascinating. He could remember times in his room above the bookstore when he tried to stay awake just so he could see an approaching storm. The window in his room faced to the west and displayed the lightning dancing over the rooftops of the city.

Once, he had been woken up by the sound of hail pelting the roof. He ran to his mother and father's room, not because he was scared, but because he wanted to go outside to collect these marbles of ice that fell from the sky. His mother discouraged the idea but could not thwart his enthusiasm, so she and his father finally consented. He ran about in the street, being pelted by hail but still managing to collect a handful of the ice pellets. They melted quickly, but not before Gabriel could examine the strange rings on them like that on the stump of a chopped-down tree. He wondered what caused these rings to form and how it was that ice fell from the sky when it was so warm outside. This was just one more of nature's strange mysteries he wanted to solve.

On this night, try as he might, Gabriel could not stay awake to view the approaching thunderstorm. The night grew dark, and the fire began to die. He heard the distant rumble of thunder as he drifted off to sleep.

He wasn't sure how long he'd been asleep, when he awoke to a loud rumble of thunder and saw another flash in the sky. He felt large drops of rain begin to fall. He grabbed his blanket and pulled it over himself as a shield from the rain. He wanted to get a good night's rest and start out early in the morning to ensure he would reach Marlborough that day. Rather than keeping him awake, the low rumble of thunder and the pattering of the rain quickly put him back into a sound sleep.

An hour or so must have passed, when a loud crack and a rushing sound awakened him. Gabriel felt wetness flowing all around him. As he began to gain his senses, he thought the rain must have been pouring down hard. It was as if he was lying in water. He then felt water flowing into his ears, over his eyes, nose, and mouth. He threw off his blanket and raised his head.

A flash of lightning illuminated the sky, and in the instant of its flash, Gabriel saw he was no longer lying on a dry, sandy beach but was now surrounded by the river. The water was rising so rapidly he felt it working its way up his chest as he sat straight up. A panic suddenly hit him, and he was fully awake. "My drum, my coins, my knife . . . where are they?"

He turned onto his hands and knees, feeling the sand beneath the ever-rising water. He couldn't see or feel anything.

The storm grew more violent. The wind creaked branches overhead, and another bolt of lightning shot from the sky.

The glow that filled the sky illuminated a small object that appeared to be floating away from him. "My drum!" he shouted. Without even thinking about the depth of the water or the force of its flow, Gabriel stamped out closer to the middle of the flowing torrent. He could now see the strap of his drum was caught on a branch sticking out of the rushing water. Bobbing up and down, it looked as if it might slide off the branch at any minute.

Gabriel walked further out toward the branch and could now feel the water trying to lift him off his feet. He reached out as far as he could, not wanting to venture any deeper. His fingertips worked their way up the stick. Stretching as far as he could, he bent the branch toward him and grabbed the strap of his drum. As he did, the stick broke. He yanked at the strap and began reeling in the drum. He had it.

Another lightning bolt crashed nearby, and Gabriel could now clearly see the danger he was in. High riverbanks surrounded him. He couldn't climb up out of the water, at least not here. But he knew he had entered the sandy beach without jumping down off a steep embankment, so he decided to try and head back upstream to the beach he had just left.

He turned and took a step back the way he'd come, but the force of the flowing water was so strong it nearly knocked him down. He knew that, no matter what, he had to keep his feet under him. If he fell and was pulled under by this flooding river, he would drown.

Gabriel saw the roots of giant oaks overhead sticking out from the banks, so he walked at an angle against the current until he reached the tangle of roots. He grabbed hold and pulled his way from one root to the next. His drum, now slung over his shoulder, bobbed along behind him. The rain still poured down, pelting his face, making it even harder to see in the darkness. He could feel the stony river bottom under his shoes and knew he had not yet reached the beach.

Standing straight up now, Gabriel realized the water had reached his chest. The more it rose, the harder it was for him to move upstream. Soon it would be over his head. He reached the last of the roots that he could grasp. As he looked up, he saw the steep embankment slope down to the water. He took one more step and felt the sandy bottom. He'd have to walk the rest of the way out without holding onto anything. Exhausted from forcing his way through the current, he took careful steps along the sandy bottom. He stumbled on something on the riverbed and began to fall, but he regained his balance by turning himself sideways to the current and spreading his legs wide.

Gabriel felt around carefully with his foot and found the object that had tripped him. Whatever it was, it was sticking straight up out of the sand. Then he realized what it could be. He remembered sticking his knife in the sand just before drifting off to sleep.

To pick it up, he would have to immerse himself in the river—something he had desperately tried to avoid. Still, a knife might be essential to his survival. Without another thought, he quickly counted to three and knelt down into the raging water.

The force of the water knocked him back as he held his breath. He hunched up into a ball and crawled forward, the glow of lightning eerily filtered through the water above him. He felt around on the ground, clouding the water with sand, which now drove into his face, pelting his skin and blocking his vision. All he could do was feel for the knife. He groped on the bottom for nearly a minute and was about ready to give up. He only hoped that when he came up for air, the water would not be over his head.

As he began to push upward off the bottom, his hand touched something. He grabbed it and shot up out of the water. He reached the surface and gasped. The water was to his chin now and sweeping his feet from under him. Desperately, he tried to reach down with his feet. As he stretched out his legs, his face tipped forward in the water. He now felt his whole body begin to float on the current. Gabriel stuck his foot down one last time. It hit the bottom and he pushed off as hard as he could and dove toward the shore.

His body splashed hard in the water. Both his feet found the sandy bottom, and again he dove forward. The water was only up to his chest now, and he clamored up and out of the water. Gasping for breath, he ran senselessly through some brush, away from the raging sound of the flooded river filling the air behind him. Branches whipped his face. Running in the darkness, not once, but twice he ran into a hard tree, which knocked him back. He regained his balance, grabbed tight to his drum, and lunged forward.

A third time, his shin hit something hard. Pain shot up his leg. He collapsed onto the wet ground, landing on some fallen branches that pushed into his gut.

Frightened but alive, he listened for the river, but all he could hear was the pelting rain through the trees. He thought of the warm bed he had at the Flemings' farm. Malinda's smile. He started to cry. He did not move again.

★ 14 ★
THE TELLING
OF THE TREASURE

Gabriel woke to birds singing overhead. His clothes were still soaked, reminding him of what had happened the night before. The sun was already high in the sky, and the air was still, humid, and heavy. He rose. His drum was still strapped around his back and swung to his side. It was dented and waterlogged but appeared to still be playable. He went to lift the strap over his head, but his hand was still grasping something. His fingers were wrapped so tightly around the object that his fingers ached. He held up his hand to his face and saw he was holding his knife. His knife! He had saved his knife. He nearly drowned, but he saved his knife. He lifted the drum strap the rest of the way off his shoulder and sat back down.

He took an inventory of what he had lost. His drumsticks must surely have been swept away. The current would also have carried away the flint rock, canteen, and fishing line. And his coin pouch . . . it would be gone. Without coppers, how could he get food to eat? Gabriel put his head between his hands and gave his thick, wet hair a yank.

"AHHHHH!" he shouted in frustration, his voice echoing through the trees. "How could I let this happen? How could I be so foolish, sleeping next to a river in a downpour?"

With the torrent gone, Gabriel slogged back through the thick underbrush in his soggy shoes until he came to the water. He found himself conjuring up hateful thoughts against the river that had taken his coins and his flint. What did a river need with coppers and a flint, anyway? The water was still covering the sandy beach, but it was not nearly as deep or swift as it had been the night before.

He stepped down into the water. It was murky. All he could do was bend over and feel around for any sign of the coin pouch. Not feeling anything, he knew if the raging river had been strong enough to sweep him off his feet, it surely had the strength to sweep away his coins. The pouch was gone, and nothing could bring it back. Gabriel kicked at the water and stood for a moment looking out over the flowing river. It didn't know or care that he had lost so much. It just flowed along as if nothing had happened.

Gabriel sloshed back out of the water and returned to his drum and knife. As he walked, he felt around in his pockets. His most precious possessions were still there. His ring. His mother's note, safe and amazingly dry from being wrapped in wax paper. And he had kept a few shillings out of his pouch that were still in his pocket. "Well," said Gabriel, "what's done is done. I can't go back and change what happened." Still, he felt foolish for having chosen to sleep so close to a shallow streambed.

He would reach Marlborough before nightfall. Along with having no coins other than the few shillings he had in his pocket, Gabriel had no food and would soon be growing hungry. He stuck his knife carefully between his ankle and his shoe, pulled the drum strap back over his shoulder, and walked back toward the road.

It was nightfall by the time he reached town. A few lights blazed from a tavern window on the main road. He had four coppers to buy enough food to make it to Cambridge. He dried off on his walk from Worcester, but he still must have looked ragged: everyone in the tavern turned to look at him as he stepped through the door.

"Come in, come in," sang a bright-faced man holding a pewter mug in each hand. Everyone returned to their business as Gabriel looked for a seat. The tavern was packed. There was only one empty chair at a table where a strange old man with a scruffy beard already sat. Gabriel tried not to stare, but he couldn't help noticing that the man had a large, wide scar that went across his entire face all the way up to his ear, which seemed to have been cut half off.

The bright-faced man set down the mugs at a wooden table surrounded by laughing men. He turned with a chortle and walked over to Gabriel. "Now, what can I bring this fine young man?" he asked, peering down into Gabriel's eyes.

"All I have is four coppers for food. Bread and dried meat would be best, as I want to return to the road yet tonight. I'm off to join the patriots." He hoped the bright-faced man would take pity and perhaps give him more to eat.

"Very well, very well . . . I'll give you a bit of fresh bread and meat for your meal tonight, and I've got some cooking bread and some scrap meat I'll pack up for you."

"The lad needs a drink, Mr. Fletcher," said the strange man sitting across from Gabriel in a gruff voice. "Bring him a mug of cider, on me."

"Very well, Mr. Tew." The bright-faced Fletcher turned to the bar.

Gabriel nodded to the stranger sitting across from him. "Thank you, sir." The man merely stared at him. He tried not to stare back at the large scar.

The two sat in silence. Mr. Fletcher returned to Gabriel with food and a mug. Gabriel was famished, but before he could take a bite, the stranger raised his mug to him without saying a word. Gabriel looked at him and slowly raised his own mug. "To you and me," said the man. "May the good Lord bless us richly."

The man clinked his mug to Gabriel's, sloshing some cider out onto the table. Then he tipped his mug up and seemed to drain the cup in one long swallow. Gabriel took a sip. It was hard cider to say the least. It was all he could do to take a sip, let alone a swallow.

"The Lord only helps them which help themselves, my boy. Ye know that, don't ye," said the stranger, slapping his mug down on the table. Before Gabriel could answer, the man went on, "Boston, Boston, that's where ye be headed, isn't it, lad? To seek fame and glory and riches. I was once a lad your age, seekin' adventures. I found mine on a ship, mind ye, a privateer's ship. Now, some folks calls us pirates, but we was always gentlemen, so we could rightly call ourselves the king's privateers. Eat now, lad. Don't ya let that fine meat go to waste."

Gabriel, without taking his eyes off the man, slowly picked up the rib of meat on his plate and gingerly took a bite, watching the man as he smiled and peered closer to him. The smell from the man's breath made Gabriel shake his head and wince.

"Do I scare ye a might?" said the man, pointing to the scar on his face. "Well, there's nothing to be scared of, laddie. I may have ran a few swords through a fair number of sailors in my day, but at heart, I be gentle as a dove."

Gabriel just nodded and took a larger bite of meat off the rib and a swig of his drink to show the stranger he was not scared of him.

"That's a fine drum ye have there. A drummer boy, are ye? I'm slick enough to figure that one, I am. We used to take a drummer boy with us on our raids at sea. Fine, brave young men, every one of 'em. Me, now, I was never a drummer boy. I had a sword and a musket in my hand since I can first remember. It was my kin's way. Thomas the Terrible is what they always called me."

"Your name is Thomas the Terrible?" asked Gabriel.

"Aye. My name is Thomas Tew the Third, to be more precise," said the man. "They call me Thomas the Terrible. I was named after my grandfather, Thomas Tew. Sailed the West Indies in the service of the king. The French and the Spaniards called him a pirate, they did. A fine man, though I never knew him. Came back to settle in Rhode Island with riches untold."

Gabriel looked in silence at Thomas. He did not look like the grandson of a wealthy man. He was dressed in rags, and Gabriel knew he could not have bathed in months. Gabriel wondered what happened to his grandfather's riches but thought better of asking. "Never talk to people about their wealth," his father would tell him.

But as if Thomas could read Gabriel's thoughts, he said, "What happened to my riches, ye ask?"

"I . . . uh . . . well," Gabriel stuttered. "No sir, I mean I didn't ask, but I was thinking about it."

"HA! A more honest lad I've yet to meet," said Thomas, almost shouting. He held up his mug to take another drink, forgetting he had already drained it with his last swig.

He slammed it down on the table, waved his hand to Mr. Fletcher, and shouted, "Get over here with more cider for me and this fine lad, Fletcher!" Gabriel had barely touched his mug but decided not to say anything.

"If I'm going to be telling ye the story of the Captain Thomas Tew and buying ye drinks, I at least ought to know your name."

Gabriel felt a little embarrassed he hadn't introduced himself. "Gabriel Cooper, sir. I'm from New York, and I'm on my way to Cambridge to join the militia as a drummer."

"Fine, fine . . . That's a fine name, Gabriel, and a gentlemen, I can tell. There's not a more worthy supper companion I could've asked for. Why, if King George III himself came to sup at this here tavern and asked to have your place at this table, I would tell him to kindly look elsewhere, Your Majesty." Thomas peered at Gabriel with a thin grin, revealing a gleaming gold tooth.

Fletcher came to the table and plopped two more mugs down. Thomas snatched his up and took a hearty gulp, shaking his head as the liquor swelled and burned from his mouth to his eyes.

"Now let me tell ye about me grandpappy, the Captain Thomas Tew. Captain Tew was a privateer most of his life and made a right fine livin' of it. He lived in the Providence Plantations all of his days and raided against French and the Spaniards from Bermuda to La Tortuga. All of the raids were under authority of the king of England, as we was at war with France and Spain. Things were good for Tew and his crew, until England made peace with Spain. Then the capture and plunder of the Spaniards vanished. Tew was left only to attack French vessels, which were many a time heavily guarded by warships and didn't have the vast treasures of the Spaniards."

Gabriel had only read of the privateers' adventures at sea. He was mesmerized by Thomas Tew's story.

"I'm not boring you now, am I, boy?" asked Thomas.

"No, sir, no. Please tell me more."

"Well then, Captain Tew heard tell of Arabian ships laden with gold, spices, and precious jewels that sailed the Indian Ocean. There were no gunboats to protect these treasure ships. He must've thought they were apples, ripe for the picking. So when the king asked Captain Tew to sail the *Amity* to raid French ships off the coast of Africa, my grandfather had another destination in mind. Instead of goin' to Africa, they could sail to the Indian Ocean, where great, unprotected riches awaited. Enough plunder to send each one of 'em home to the colonies never to have to work again. My grandfather, rest his soul, was a great leader. Every one of those crewmen agreed to head to the Indian Ocean in disregard of the king's mission to Africa. It's that same ambitious spirit—not bein' afraid of a high and mighty king—that's drivin' this here war, if you ask me," said Thomas, raising his mug once more.

After taking a swig, he continued, "It was off to the Indian Ocean that the *Amity* sailed. Word is they spent months looking for this promised Arabian treasure. The crew was surely gettin' agitated at Captain Tew, but he kept 'em to the task and, sure enough, the very day they agreed to turn the *Amity's* sails homeward, the promised bounty of gold was before their eyes. The Arabian ship they were after had departed from the Red Sea, loaded with treasure beyond belief. Captain Tew needed only to fire a few warnin' blasts from his cannon before the treasure ship surrendered its cargo. And oh, the riches to be found," said Thomas with his eyes twinkling in a dreamy state.

"What was it?" asked Gabriel, trying to snap Thomas back to attention.

"Gabriel, me lad, there was precious jewels of rubies, sapphires, emeralds, and pearls; there were fine silks and spices worth thousands of the king's sterling; and then there was gold and silver—more gold and silver than you can imagine. They took all that plunder back to the island of Madagascar, off the coast of Africa, where they split it up fair and square among the crew. There was so much to go 'round not one man complained of his take. The crew sailed back home to Rhode Island in 1694, and Captain Tew was given a hero's welcome. He built a big house, enjoyed the company of important people, and raised his family, which included my father, the son of Captain Tew his self."

Here, Thomas paused and drained the mug then set it firmly back on the table. Gabriel was enthralled by the story, but his question about what happened to the treasure had been left unanswered. "What happened to all the treasure?" he asked timidly.

Thomas sat across the table, looking at Gabriel intently, and did not say a word. Gabriel wondered if maybe he should not have asked that question, since Thomas had a strange look in his eye. Softly, almost whispering, Thomas said, "Gabriel, a keen lad you are, indeed. Most boys your age would have been so lost in my story of pirates and plunder and treasure they would have forgotten all about the question at hand. You, however, are different than most boys your age. You want to know what happened to the treasure, do ye? Your honesty and keenness should be rewarded, so I'll tell you what happened to Captain Tew's treasure. But only if you swear a solemn oath on the holy word of God should you find the missin' treasure, you'll return half of it to me, its rightful owner."

Mysteriously, Thomas the Terrible produced from his coat pocket a small Bible, which he set before Gabriel. Gabriel sat stunned, questions swirling in his head. Thomas the Terrible carried a Bible? His grandfather's treasure was missing, and Gabriel might be able to find it? Was the treasure nearby? Why hadn't Thomas found it? Coming to his senses, he slid his hand over on top of Thomas' Bible and said, "I swear."

"Very well, now where was we," said Thomas with a strange lightness in his voice.

"The treasure?" responded Gabriel.

"Gabriel, me lad, if ye be thinkin' Captain Tew spent it all, then you're dead wrong. One man could not have spent all that wealth in one lifetime, even if he tried. But riches can be a poison that seeps slowly through a person's veins until they've lost all sense of themselves. Captain Tew, I believe, had a bit of that poison in him, for he began thinkin' everyone was out to steal his money. He kept most of it locked up in a safe, and he sat by it day and night. Then one day, Captain Tew got the idea that the best thing to do was to use his money to buy up as much land as he could. His thinkin' was that no one can steal land. Once you own the title to it, it's yours. But it was this quest for land that led to Captain Tew's demise.

"Captain Tew heard there was good land for sale north in Massachusetts, so one fine October day, he set out alone on horseback with a good chunk of his gold and silver in a sack. He was goin' to make a huge land purchase. He insisted on traveling alone so no one would know what he was up to. He was to meet a man in Boston to complete the purchase, so he traveled along this very road that you're travelin' on, Gabriel.

"He was not far from Boston when bandits attacked. Captain Tew was not one to give up without a fight. He ran one of the bandits through with his sword and burst into the underbrush of the woods to escape the others. He rode until he came to the Charles River and soon realized he couldn't cross. So he rode up the river and reached the foot of a steep cliff, where a waterfall came flowing and crashing down upon the rocks in front of him. He climbed off his horse and grabbed his bag of gold and silver, slingin' it o'er his back. The bandits rode up and saw him tryin' to escape. They fired their muskets at him as he scaled the rocky cliff, but Tew reached the top unharmed.

"The bag of gold and silver now weighed heavy on his shoulder, and he knew he could not continue much longer with the bag of treasure. So he found a giant oak tree near the bank of the Charles River with a hollow at the base of its tangled roots. Captain Tew stuck the bag inside and carved a letter 'T' in the trunk with his sword. All of this took time, and that's all the bandits needed to find a path around the steep cliff up to where he now stood. On horseback, they stamped up to him, their muskets drawn to shoot, but one of them noticed Captain Tew no longer had his sack of treasure. My grandfather keenly told them he had thrown it into the river, and then he jumped in his self before the bandits knew what to do. My poor grandfather was carried away by the swift current toward the waterfall. As he looked behind, he saw the bandits enter the river on horseback, looking for the treasure. Then he toppled over the waterfall, where he was dashed upon the rocks.

"He was found by a traveler, washed up on the banks o' the Charles a day or so later. He was still alive, but just barely. They took Captain Tew to a doctor in Boston, who was unable to save him. Many years later in my search for his treasure, I found that doctor and asked him what my grandfather told him. The old doctor told me the story I just told you. It was one of the most amazin' deathbed stories he had ever heard. The doctor counted it as mindless jibber from a dying man, but I know better, Gabriel. I know Captain Tew hid his treasure in the hollow of a giant oak tree near the banks of the Charles, just upstream from a waterfall."

"You've surely looked for it?" asked Gabriel.

"Aye, I've looked for it, Gabriel, but I haven't found it. As for the rest of the treasure Captain Tew left, my father squandered it on ships, liquor, and women. There was but a little left for me, and I can't say I've fared much better than my father."

Gabriel felt sorry for the ragged man sitting in front of him.

"Gabriel, I'm gettin' too old to be tromping around lookin' for treasure. I've even changed some of my terrible ways in my old age, which is why I carry the Holy Scriptures with me. I've been waitin' for some time now to find someone who I might tell this to. I don't know what it is, but I sense the good Lord has sent you here to sit at this table and hear this story. It may be you're meant to look for the treasure."

Gabriel nodded his head. "I could look for the treasure on my way, but I can't be delayed too long. I may have already missed my chance to join the militia."

"The Charles River," said Thomas, "nears the road about a day's walk from Marlborough. You can hear it from the road. When ye do hear it, leave the road and follow it north. I have seen more than one waterfall, but I haven't been able to explore them all.

"There's one more thing you should know. While no one but me and you knows the true story about my grandfather, there's still plenty o' legends 'bout his death. Most people think he was struck down and killed by the bandits who stole away with his treasure, and so they say the ghost of Thomas Tew walks the banks of the Charles River at night with his sword in hand, looking for revenge. I tell you this not to scare ye lad, but just so ye know."

Gabriel shuddered at this thought and wished Thomas had not told him this part of the story. What if Thomas the Terrible was as crazy as he looked? But what if he wasn't, and there really was treasure?

Well, he thought, *I've heard this strange story for some reason, treasure or not, and I'm headed to Boston. What harm could there be in looking for this poor man's lost treasure along the way?*

"I will look for it," said Gabriel, smiling.

"A good lad, ye are," responded Thomas. "A good lad . . . and don't worry nothin' about that ghost."

★ 15 ★

THE GHOST
OF THOMAS TEW

Thunder crashed outside the small window of the tavern. Gabriel saw the flash of lightning and the rain pelting down. He dreaded heading out into the storm. As he savored the last bites of meat and bread, he decided to wait inside the tavern until the owner told him he must leave.

Thomas had dozed off, his head face-down on the table. After finishing his food, Gabriel dozed off, too, but was not sure how long he had been asleep when Fletcher came up to him and shook him awake. "Lad, here's the dried meat and bread I promised you. I've let you stay here till the storm cleared outside, but I need to lock up now, and you need to be on your way."

Gabriel yawned and stretched. Looking across, he could see Thomas. He was snoring, still face-down on the table. Fletcher leaned over to shake Thomas now. "Wake up, Tew, wake up!" he shouted, much more abruptly than he had dealt with Gabriel. "Time for you to move on now."

Thomas stuttered and spat, then rose up from the table in a complete stupor, patted Gabriel on the back, gave him a wink, and without saying a word, walked out the door. Still groggy, Gabriel took the pack from the owner and tried to determine the weight of its contents. It didn't seem too heavy, and he only hoped it would be enough to get him through to Boston now that he had no money. That, of course, could all change with Thomas Tew's treasure.

Gabriel stepped out into the night. A light rain fell, and he could see a few flashes of lightning lingering in the east. The rainwater ponded all along the road, and Gabriel knew they must have just gotten another torrential downpour. The Charles River would be up, he was sure of that.

He was tired and needed to sleep. There was a small covered porch on the front of the tavern. He would stay put and curl up out of the rain. *The tavern owner won't mind*, he thought.

He fell asleep quickly, but the morning sun seemed to rise just as fast. He rubbed his still-tired eyes and stretched his stiff bones.

He was close now. He could feel it. Only one day's walk to the river, and then another day or two before he would be looking for Nathaniel Greene and his band of Rhode Island militia. Not wanting to waste any more time in Marlborough, he set off down the road. As he strode out of town, he wondered where Thomas the Terrible had taken off to last night.

Gabriel had gone out the door of the tavern just a minute behind Thomas, but there was no sign of the man. *He must have a house some place nearby,* he thought.

The more distance Gabriel put between himself and Marlborough, the stranger the man's story seemed to him. It was like waking from a dream that at first seems real, but begins to fade the longer you're awake. He was having doubts about whether he should really follow through on his promise to look for the treasure on his way to Boston. What if it took him so far out of his way that he ran out of food? He was already hungry from his morning of walking, so he stopped off the road for a bite to eat. Peering into the small cloth bag, he saw how meager his provisions really were. The food would only last a few days, and that would be stretching it.

Gabriel took some nourishment, found a small pool of fresh rainwater to drink from, and set back down the road. If he didn't hear the sound of the river along the road as Thomas said he would, he would not stray from the path to look for the treasure. Just as he made this decision, the faint sound of gurgling water came to his ear. He almost wished he hadn't heard it, but there it was, growing louder with every step.

It was late afternoon. He stood in the road, listening to the unmistakable sound of rushing water. He knew what he had told Thomas the Terrible, and he couldn't back away now. He had to leave the road and follow the river. He stepped off the path into a densely wooded area with enormous trees that created an interwoven canopy of leaves and branches. He turned and took one last look at the road—the road that would take him to Cambridge where the militia was camped. Then he turned back to the dark woods and strode ahead toward the sound of flowing water.

Passing under the canopy of green overhead, Gabriel found the river, swollen and nearly cresting its banks. He would have to bushwhack along the river, as brush, bramble, and vines were growing on the forest floor beneath the canopy of the large trees. He paused for a moment to take in the different kinds of trees—walnut, hickory, sycamore, cherry, poplar, some pine, and numerous large oak. How would he ever find a single oak with a "T" carved in the bark?

Walking along the river, Gabriel pressed his way through the brush, sometimes needing to take out his knife to cut away at some thorn bushes blocking his path. He was thankful he had saved his knife and drum but still lamented the fact that he lost nearly everything else in the raging river. Was this the same river that had stolen his coins in the flood? Was this the river Thomas the Terrible meant? Would it take him to Cambridge as Thomas claimed?

Gabriel walked along the river's edge the rest of the afternoon. Making slow progress, he came across two very small waterfalls that only dropped a few feet. There was no steep cliff to scale, so he quickly dismissed any thought that these would be the waterfalls where Captain Tew left his treasure.

The branches overhead blocked out so much sunlight, it was hard to tell what time of day it was. Still, Gabriel sensed the night. He relished the thought of a bright fire. Then he realized he didn't have his flint rock with him. "Blast!" he said out loud.

He yearned for a warm fire as he shivered at even the thought of the coming cold, dark night in the middle of this dense wood. He had spent other nights on his journey without a fire, but none so far from the road in such a dense forest—one sure to hold panthers, bears, wolves, and coyotes. The hazy green light quickly gave way to darkness, and a cool mist seemed to rise from the forest floor. He didn't even have a blanket to wrap around him. He felt naked. It was as if the forest was closing thick claws around him that would not unclench until morning came. With the white mist wafting in the air, visible only with the last glimpses of light, a thought crept into Gabriel's mind: *What about the ghost of Thomas Tew?*

"Stop thinking about that nonsense," he scolded himself. "There's no such thing as the ghost of Thomas Tew."

Still, he wished Thomas the Terrible had not mentioned anything about his grandfather's ghost roaming the woods, sword drawn, looking for the bandits who tried to steal his treasure. *Well,* thought Gabriel, *I'm not a bandit, so what would he want with me, anyway?*

Gabriel arranged some pine needles into a bed and laid down. There was only a sliver of moon, and what light it and the stars may have provided, the ceiling of branches and leaves above mostly hid. It was dark now. He couldn't even see his hand as he held it in front of his face. Gabriel felt around on the ground. He had his drum beside him and clutched his knife in his hand.

As Gabriel lay in the darkness, he began to hear the soft hooting of an owl. He listened closely. At first, he could hear just the faint *"hoo-hoo,"* but the sound was growing louder now. As he listened, the owl's voice seemed to change. He sat up in his bed now and listened, *"Tewww, Tewww. . . . Tewww, Tewww,"* came the call from the woods not far away. Then Gabriel heard a branch crack on the forest floor, several yards away from his bed. He peered into the darkness, trying to figure out what had made the cracking sound. He sat straight up, all of his senses at attention.

"Tewwww, Tewwww . . . Tewwww, Tewwww," came to Gabriel's ears again, and then another crack of a branch, this time closer.

He clenched his drum in one hand and his knife in the other. Something was in the woods, watching him. He could feel its presence. He heard another crack, again closer. He stood up, his knife in front of him. A sudden gust of wind split the still of the night, parting the branches overhead just enough to let a glimmer of light down upon the forest floor. He saw a white, wispy figure curling through the night air flying toward him. At that instant, the branches closed again, and Gabriel heard a loud crack just a few feet away. He swung his knife blindly in front of him, but he heard another loud crack even closer. Feeling the mist beginning to wrap around him, he turned and ran.

He ran as fast as he could through the forest, without knowing where he was going. As he ran, he thought he heard the snapping of branches in the darkness behind him. He felt his heart beating and heard his breath, fast and heavy, in the night air. No matter how far he ran, he still felt as if he was being followed.

He tried to speed up, but he was growing winded. Around him, he could hear the wind picking up again and the branches creaking loudly overhead. He was too terrified to turn and look behind him. Running blindly through the thick wood and bramble, Gabriel felt the sting of thorns tearing at his legs, branches whipping his face and arms. A thick vine grabbed his ankle, and he stumbled over some rocks. Unable to break his fall, he landed hard, slamming his head onto the forest floor.

★16★

THE WATERFALL

When Gabriel next opened his eyes, sunlight was warming his face. As he moved his head, it throbbed with pain. He heard the roaring sound of water. Finally, he stood and looked through a clearing in the trees. The river water cascaded down a steep cliff at least thirty feet high. It crashed onto the rocks below before churning in a bubbly foam down the river.

Gabriel wasn't sure how he'd ended up there. The last thing he remembered was being chased by what he thought was the ghost of Thomas Tew. He looked at the rocky cliffs on either side of the waterfall and could picture Captain Tew climbing, carrying his sack of gold and silver and bandits taking aim with their muskets. "This has to be it," he said aloud.

Dizziness hit him then, and Gabriel sat down on a rock not far from the churning water. His head was still aching. *Maybe some food would do me good,* he thought. He only had enough meat and bread left for a meager breakfast. He hated to eat everything he had left, especially since the prospects of finding more seemed slim, but knew it would help his dizziness. So he ate.

He sat alone in the sunny clearing and dreamed about the Fleming farm for a moment. He wondered what Malinda, Constance, and Mr. Fleming were doing. His time on their farm seemed so long ago. They had probably just finished a fine breakfast of pancakes and sausage. He could almost smell the sausage sizzling on the griddle. Malinda's words came to his mind. "You have a vision for your life that's more than this simple farm can offer," she had said. He remembered the pride in her eyes as she urged him to press on, saying, "I will pray for your safe return." He had work to do before he could ever return to the Fleming farm.

With food in his belly, Gabriel's mind began to clear, but what had happened the night before was still a mystery. He had no idea what might have been chasing him, if anything at all. Had he run from nothing but a fictitious ghost created by his overactive imagination? Had it been some forest animal? He would never know, but the one thing he was sure of was that he did not want to spend another night in these woods.

Although he now stood before a waterfall matching the story of Thomas Tew, doubts raced through Gabriel's mind. Reaching Cambridge and joining the patriot cause meant far more to him than finding hidden treasure ever could. Still, he was here, and he had no better ideas on which way to go in this wilderness.

He slowly walked along the rocky shore to the base of the falls. The cliff on either side was covered with pointed rocks jutting out in all directions. There were also a few small trees growing out from the rocks here and there on the face of the cliff. Gabriel walked over to the cliff, mapping his ascent. He put one hand on a rock above and put his foot on a rock just out in front. As he tried to lift himself up, his hand slipped, and he fell backward. He brushed himself off and went back to examine the rocks more closely. They were all covered with a slippery green moss. Without rope, climbing the cliff would be impossible.

He thought for a moment and remembered Thomas had told him the bandits found a way up on horseback. "There must be another way," muttered Gabriel. He left the sunny clearing and began tromping through the woods. Reentering the dense forest made him uncomfortable again, even in the daytime. He walked along the base of the cliff, which seemed to extend as far as he could see into the woods. Maybe the bandits and Captain Tew were on the other side of the river? There was no way he could get across the river when it was still so high. The thought of entering a raging river again gave him goose bumps.

He walked for almost an hour in one direction along the base of the cliff. He found nothing. "Enough of this!" Gabriel felt foolish for wasting the morning chasing after the legend of an old drunk.

But just as he turned to head back down the river, he noticed a particularly thick patch of bushes growing out of the cliff. He took out his knife and cut away at some of the branches. He reached his hand into the bushes, trying to feel where they came out of the cliff. But to his astonishment, there didn't seem to be any cliff behind the bushes.

He began stomping down the bushes with his feet and stabbing at the branches with his knife. Once he was through the thickest part, he could see a sloped trail set out before him. Gabriel's heart leapt at finding this passageway hidden by the overgrowth of bushes. The path was still rocky and steep, but it was an easy climb compared to the cliff on either side of him.

He pawed his way along the path, still having to trudge through weeds and bushes before he finally reached the top. He stepped out into sunlight and saw the river. The water raced along at a mesmerizing pace before disappearing over the rushing falls ahead. He watched a large fallen branch floating along the current. It met the edge of the fall and dropped instantly out of view.

What a horrible way to die, thought Gabriel. If what Thomas the Terrible had told him was true, his grandfather met a horrible fate toppling over the edge of that waterfall.

The sun was still high in the sky but making its way down now. He left the edge of the waterfall and headed further upstream. The river bent gently to the left and disappeared out of sight. Gabriel walked along the bank as close to the water as he could without risking a fall into the swift current.

The water had gone down a little from its recent highs, so he could see the effects of the powerful flow of water that had gushed through the river. At more than one spot along the bank, slender young sapling trees, several feet tall, had been snapped in two by the force of the water. Other young trees had their roots exposed, just waiting for a good wind to topple them over into the river.

Where the river began to bend, large boulders jutted out from the water, creating frothy foam all around them. The water swirled to and fro as it darted around one rock and then another. In most places, only the very tops of the rock peeked up out of the swirling water.

Gabriel turned his attention back to trees. There was no guarantee the oak tree he was looking for would still be standing. After all, it was at least a hundred years old. So he tried to take careful notice of the trees that had fallen and were decaying on the forest floor. This made his job even more difficult, for a maple tree decaying on the forest floor looks the same as an oak. He noticed the beginning of a narrow trail leading away from the bend in the river. *Maybe Captain Tew didn't pick a tree right on the bank of the river,* he thought.

Gabriel decided to follow the trail. He walked the entire length and, in a matter of a few minutes, found himself back at the river, only now well upstream from the bend. *This trail is nothing more than a shortcut used by deer or other animals coming to the river to drink,* he realized. There were very few oak trees along the trail, and the ones there didn't have any hollows with hidden treasure inside.

Even more frustrated than before, Gabriel walked a little bit further upstream to a small clearing beside the river. Exhausted, he plopped down on a large rock very near the river's edge. Why had he listened to the crazy ranting of an old drunk who looked like a common beggar?

He thought about getting back to the road, but he no longer knew how to find the road. Now he was out of coins and food, and this forest seemed to be an uninhabited waste-land. There would be little chance of him stumbling across a house. Gabriel's stomach growled. He could already begin to feel the first twinges of a hunger he knew would not go away. It would only grow worse. He put his head in his hands and prayed. It was the only thing he could think of to do at the moment.

With his head in his hands, Gabriel sat motionless on the rock. He knew to look up would mean facing the foreboding circumstance surrounding him. He looked down at the drum resting at his feet and cursed the day he found it and pulled it out of the muddy banks of the East River back in New York. Yet, it had become a part of him. It was silly, really, he thought. He didn't even know how to play the thing other than to bang it, making a senseless noise. Yet, the idea of being a drummer boy in the militia had brought him a long way from New York.

Finally, he raised his head to look around him. The sun had set just a bit lower in the sky, casting shadows of the large trees over the river. Gabriel realized he would be spending another night here in the woods. The thought sent a chill down his spine. He was not really sure what he'd seen last night in its misty form, but he knew he didn't want to see it again.

Still a little dizzy from the blow he received the night before, Gabriel's vision blurred as he stood to look upstream. The river made another bend several hundred yards further upstream. Dense woods lined it the entire way. As he peered along the bank, one of the trees caught Gabriel's eyes, as if it had just appeared out of nowhere. It was taller than all of the rest of the trees along that portion of the bank, and it looked like an oak. He stepped out onto the rock to get a little better look. What he saw startled him. A gnarled entanglement of large roots on the ground around the tree appeared to have formed a hollow just at the base of the giant oak. Gabriel's heart leapt up into his throat. He knew this had to be the tree where the treasure was hidden.

★ 17 ★

THE JOURNEY ENDS

Gabriel gathered up his drum and began to turn around to leap back onto the bank and make a mad rush for the tree. Just as he turned, something in the river caught his eye. A dark object appeared to be moving in the shadowy water, coming around the bend in the river upstream from him. He stood motionless on the rock, straining his eyes to see. Looking more closely, he could see the something moving or waving.

The thought of Thomas Tew's ghost crept into Gabriel's mind, sending chills up and down his back again. But this was not the white phantom shape he had seen the other night. Still, he thought it was odd the shape had appeared in the water just as he spotted the giant hollowed oak tree. This being—or whatever it was—had sprung up in the river at the exact spot where Captain Tew would have jumped in to escape the bandits' musket fire. In fear, disbelief, or perhaps exhaustion, a sudden fainting spell caught hold of him. His vision blurred again, and he lost his balance, almost stumbling off the rock and into the river.

Squatting to his knees, Gabriel again looked upriver. He heard something above the sound of rushing water and the low drone of the waterfall that lay downstream. He thought he heard someone calling out. Again, he heard the noise. He was able now to hear a muffled, "Help me . . ."

Gabriel forced himself to look up at the shape floating down the river. His vision cleared enough to see what looked like a man waving one arm. His other arm was wrapped around a small log, as he struggled to stay afloat. The current swept him along. This did not look, or sound, like a ghost.

Gabriel could now hear the cries more clearly. "HELP! HELP!" The man let go of the log and grasped at a boulder that barely broke the surface of the frothy water. He caught hold and clung on. Then he turned toward Gabriel and looked him squarely in the eyes. Venturing to the edge of the rock on the river's bank, Gabriel looked closely now. The man had a gash on his forehead, and blood was oozing from the cut.

That's no ghost, Gabriel thought. Instinctively, he began to move more quickly. His mind cleared as his adrenaline raced. Again, he thought of how Thomas Tew met his death tumbling over the approaching waterfall. He waved at the man from the rock. "Hold on," he shouted. Gabriel leapt from the rock to the bank and turned to head upstream to where the man had caught hold of the boulder. But as soon as he turned, the man lost his grip on the boulder and began careening down the tumbling water once more.

Gabriel began to panic. What could he do for this man? The stranger would soon float past him. He knew he could certainly not jump into the river to try to save the man.

His mind raced. He must find some way to get him out. The man was growing near, his head still above the water, arms flailing. "The trail," Gabriel said to himself. He could take the shortcut at the bend. If he ran, he might be able to get ahead of the man and throw something for him to grab on to.

He turned and sprinted back to the narrow trail, his drum catching on the brush as he ran. He lifted the strap over his shoulder and threw it to the ground. He ran as fast as he had the night before when he was running for his own life. This time, it was the life of the man in the river he was running to save.

Gabriel burst out at the trailhead. The raging sound of the waterfall was much louder now, almost drowning out his thoughts. He quickly went to the bank and looked upstream. The man was still being swept along by the current. Gabriel had gotten ahead of him, but now what?

He surveyed his surroundings, looking for something to throw the drowning man. If he could find a long enough fallen tree limb, he could toss it out and pull the man to shore. He scrambled along the bank, pushing old leaves aside on the forest floor, but there were no long limbs to be found.

Then Gabriel spotted a tall, slender sapling with exposed roots on the muddy bank from the rushing waters. If he could topple this sapling, it might be long enough to reach the man. He ran at the sapling, slamming all of his weight into it at once. The young tree bent but did not fall. Again Gabriel ran at the tree, forcing one of its roots to give way. He was surprised by the strength of the tree.

"May God have mercy!" the man shouted, growing closer now. Gabriel again slammed his body into the tree and then took it by the trunk, rocking it back and forth. He kicked at it, punched at it. Still, it would not fall. He could see the man clearly now. Seeing what Gabriel was trying to do, the man began flailing his arms in order to push himself closer to where Gabriel struggled with the tree. Gabriel ran back a good twenty yards. He turned, sprinted, and jumped at the tree just before he reached the base, sending all of his rushing weight at the center of the sapling. A cracking sound filled the air, and he rolled onto his side, nearly falling into the water.

The tree finally toppled into the river. The top of it had been dragged downstream a few feet, where it lodged against a boulder. The base of the tree remained attached to the riverbank by a few straggly, thin roots. Although the current tugged at the tree, its roots held fast.

Gabriel looked up from the muddy ground, his face only a few inches from the edge of the bank that fell into the river. The man was trying with all his might to reach the tree lying in the river. He flailed his arms, just making it to the boulder and banging up against it with a sudden force. Then he flung himself off the boulder onto the slender tree. Pulling himself along the tree, he slowly crawled to the bank where Gabriel lay. Gabriel could now see he was middle-aged and had no doubt been weakened by the struggle in the river.

The man reached the bank, but with blood still coming from his forehead, he could not pull himself up out of the water. Himself exhausted, Gabriel stumbled to his feet and held out his hand to the man. The man weakly grasped hold of Gabriel's arm just below the elbow. Gabriel pulled, but the man did not budge. He dug his feet in and pulled again. This time, the man rose up onto the bank.

Losing his balance from the force of the man pulling his arm, Gabriel's feet slipped in the mud. He tried to grasp hold of something, but there was nothing to grab, and he plummeted into the river.

The force of the cold river water took Gabriel's breath away. His head went under. Blindly reaching up, he groped aimlessly. Miraculously, his hand found the tree. Grabbing hold, he began to pull himself up. He got his head up to grab a breath, but in his exhaustion, he was not able to keep his head above the water. Gabriel could feel himself beginning to slip away. His grip was loosening on the tree, his last connection to life fading.

★18★

FOUND

Gabriel felt himself falling. He could picture himself hurtling over the waterfall, down to the rocks below. His jacket went tight on his chest, but rather than the sensation of falling he expected, he felt as if he was being lifted. The pressure of the water no longer pressed him to continue to try to hold his breath. He exhaled with great force as a feeling of weightlessness filled his senses, but he couldn't inhale. His body was thrown down onto something hard. Something like a mallet started beating on his chest.

He coughed and spewed water from his lungs and stomach and tried to draw a breath but couldn't. Again he coughed and vomited. He gasped, desperate for air, and then it came. The air filled his lungs as he took a breath and then another. He continued to cough, but his breath had returned.

Someone was beside him and helped him to sit up. He could not see, but he heard the pounding of the waterfall and the whinny of a horse.

Then a voice came. "You're going to be all right, just try to relax."

Gabriel turned his head toward the voice. "Who's there?"

"No questions, at least not yet. Just rest," came a strong but quiet voice. Gabriel lay back down and rested.

A while later, he was not awake but not quite asleep when he overheard men talking. The same voice that told him to rest said, "You know, Artemas, you are one lucky man to be sitting here alive. After your horse threw you off when we were crossing the river, you plunged into that swirling water and, I hate to say it, but I thought I had seen the last of you."

"I wouldn't call it luck," replied a weak-voiced man. "More like divine intervention. For this boy to be standing along the bank of the river, see me coming, somehow get ahead of me, and then have brains and courage to pluck me out, it must be one of His miracles. By the grace of God, I owe the young man my life."

"How did he do it?" questioned a third man with a deep and clear voice.

"I'm not sure," said Artemas. "First time I saw him was when I grabbed onto a boulder in the middle of the river, but the current was too strong, I couldn't hold on. When I turned back to look for the lad, he was gone. Next thing I know, I see him up ahead of me, jumping at a tree. It falls over and lodges perfectly against a rock in the river. I was able to grab a hold of the tree and pull myself to the shore, but I didn't have the strength to pull myself up out of the river. That's when the boy reached down and, bless his courageous soul, tugged on me so hard his foot slipped, and in he went. I reached for him, but I was so weak I was near to useless. My heart sank to think about my young savior meeting the doom meant for me. I saw his head bob up for a moment. He managed to grab the tree, but then his head went back under, and I didn't see him again. Not until good ole' Nate here rode up, ran over, and plucked that boy up like a fish on a hook."

"That was well done," came the clear, deep voice again.

"It was nothing, Your Excellency—nothing compared to what this young man did to save the life of Artemas Greenwood."

The man with the deep, clear voice chuckled, "Excellency! That's what you call me now, is it? I must admit, I'm not quite used to that title. General Washington will do when we are out in the field together."

"I will try to remember, sir, but having been placed in command over all the troops around Boston, 'Your Excellency' is what Joseph Reed told us to call you."

"Yes, yes, I know . . . I know. And Reed is a good aide; yet, the burden of this undertaking is already heavy enough. I don't know whether to call John Adams a friend or the devil for convincing Congress I should be commander over this rabble of men that thinks itself an army."

"Well, I didn't mean it in a bad way, Your Excellency—I mean . . . General. There are plenty of men with ambitious spirits, hungry for power, who would give anything to be called the supreme commander of our army."

"Yes, I know you are right. I do cherish this honor, but with honor comes an enormous responsibility. You surely realize this. How are we to drive the regulars from Boston? We have no navy, these militias are disorganized, and many of these men are sick, wounded, or have little ammunition. Franklin even suggested we arm them with arrow and bow. And we have precious few cannon. I would be lying if I didn't tell you my heart is overwhelmed sometimes, and its only desire is to return to Mount Vernon, the hills of Virginia, and Martha."

Artemas responded, his voice sounding a bit stronger, "Well, General Washington, we must convince the men at Cambridge you are the man who can drive Howe's redcoats from Boston. I believe it, and soon everyone will."

Gabriel stirred a little. He had heard everything and, at first, thought it was a dream. Could it really be he was in the presence of the commander over all the troops at Cambridge? This was the general whom Charlie the innkeeper spoke of back in Springfield. This man would surely know where to find Nathaniel Greene.

Gabriel was afraid to fully wake, for fear the voices would vanish and he would be left alone again in these terrible woods. His vision had returned, and he saw the fading sunlight, bright against three shadowy figures next to him.

Looking into the sun, squinting his eyes, he caught glimpse of the men before him. They were handsome in their finely tailored uniforms—blue-tailed coats faced in buff, with gold epaulettes. He sat up. He was in the presence of officers who certainly could take him to camp near Cambridge, where he could look for Nathaniel Greene.

"Well, it looks like our young hero is awake," came the voice of the man they called His Excellency, General Washington.

"Well, young man, do you feel up for a ride?" asked the rider Artemas had called Nate. "We'd like to get back to camp before it's too late, and we'll likely be needing to drop you off at your home. I'm sure your ma's worried sick about you."

Nate's words about dropping him off at home surprised Gabriel. These men didn't know how far he'd come to join the militia. But why should they? To them, he was just a boy who happened to be along the river when this militiaman named Artemas Greenwood came rolling down the current. It struck him as a little funny that everyone along his travels knew where he was heading, but now that he was finally at his jour-ney's end, these soldiers didn't recognize what he was up to.

"Can you tell us where your folks are, lad? I can put you on the back of my horse and have you home lickity split," said Nate, trying to work a response out of Gabriel.

Gabriel responded, his tongue thick in his mouth. "I haven't got a home, sir."

"Well, I certainly understand that," said General Washington. "We all feel like we're homeless, being so far away from our families. Tell me now, though, where are your mother and father, son?"

"I don't have a mother or father, sir," replied Gabriel.

"I'm sorry," said the general, surprised. "Could you please repeat that, son?"

"My mother and father died of the pox a little over a year ago. We had a home, but it got sold to pay off debts. My mother was from France and my father from England. I don't have any living relatives," said Gabriel plainly.

"Where did you come from, then?" asked Nate.

"New York, sir," replied Gabriel.

"Good Lord!" came a shout from Artemas.

"New York?" all three men questioned at once in disbelief. "How did you get here?"

"I walked," said Gabriel.

Washington cleared his throat and began, "Young man, I must be blunt with you. I find this story very hard to believe. You are how old?"

"I'm twelve, sir . . . almost thirteen."

"What is your name, son?" questioned Washington.

"Gabriel Cooper, sir."

"Can you please explain why you have walked nearly two hundred and fifty miles, all the way from New York to Cambridge?" asked Washington.

"I . . . well, sir, I wanted to join the militia. I thought I could be a drummer boy," replied Gabriel.

"That would explain this, then," said General Washington, reaching down beside him and holding up something to the other men. It appeared to be Gabriel's drum, but it looked funny—misshapen somehow. "I found this," continued Washington, looking to Nate, "when I was chasing after you on that trail. Or, should I say, my horse found it."

Then Gabriel viewed just enough of the drum in the dim light to see it must have been stepped on by General Washington's horse. It had a dent in the side, and part of the drumskin on top had been torn away.

"My drum!" exclaimed Gabriel, unable to control himself. "My drum . . . I . . . how can I . . .?"

"I'm sorry, young master Gabriel," responded General Washington. "I certainly did not intend to step on it, and I would gladly repair it. But, honestly, I think it is beyond repair. You must be quite a drummer boy if this drum is so dear to your heart. It's too bad we could not hear you play it."

In an instant, Gabriel's troubles over losing his drum vanished, and he had to fight back laughter. If these men only knew what kind of drummer boy he really was. Just like that, he realized how fortunate it was that his drum had been destroyed. Its destruction had saved him the embarrassment of being asked to retrieve some sticks from the wood and beat out a tune. The tune, of course, would have been unrecognizable banging that would have certainly made a very poor impression, if not hurt the ears of those listening.

"It's all right about the drum," said Gabriel. "It just meant a lot to me because it came with me all the way from New York. I still want to stay and fight the redcoats, even without my drum."

"Gabriel . . . I don't think we can allow that," said General Washington. "You are only twelve years old, and how do I know you aren't telling us a tall tale about journeying from New York to Boston? As far as I know, you may just live around the bend in the river."

Gabriel was hurt by these words. Why shouldn't these men believe him? After all, he just saved one of their lives.

The man named Nate spoke up. "Gabriel, surely you understand why we're struggling to accept all you've told us as true. It's not that we think you're untrustworthy. It's just . . ."

Gabriel's head was spinning. He lost track of what Nate was saying, and he couldn't believe what he was hearing. He had walked all the way from New York to Boston by himself and, now he'd reached the very people who could make him part of the militia, they didn't believe him. "No! I don't understand why you don't believe me," he blurted out rather sternly. "What must I do to make you believe me? I can tell you every town I stopped at along the way; I can tell you about being chased down and kicked by lobsterbacks at

King's Bridge; I saw ships—Royal Navy ships—in the sound. I can tell you about falling ill and being nursed back to health by the Flemings in New Haven. And Mr. Arnold—I spoke to Colonel Benedict Arnold! His voice had risen to almost a shout. The frustration in him was welling up like a volcano ready to blow.

Artemas broke in, "Now . . . now, Nathaniel, let the boy have a chance to speak before we dismiss him out of hand. He did save my life, after all. What would your dear wife, Caty, say if she knew how you were treating an orphan? She might not have wanted to marry a Greene, after all. Besides, I've brought my boy Jonathon with me to Cambridge. He's only twelve."

Gabriel heard the words come from Artemas, but it took him a while to understand their significance. The men continued chattering in the background about what to do with Gabriel while his mind raced. If *Nate* was short for *Nathaniel* . . . and his wife, Caty, had married a Greene . . . this man was Nathaniel Greene. Without even thinking, he shouted out, "NATHANIEL GREENE!"

The men stopped talking and looked curiously at Gabriel. Nate looked closely at him and said, "Yes, I am Nathaniel Greene."

This was the man he was told to seek out when he reached Boston, but this was also the very man who didn't believe he had walked all the way from New York. Gabriel's thoughts floated away, back to the King's Bridge Tavern at the very beginning of his journey, where he met Ben Daniels and was told to look for Nathaniel Greene when he reached Boston. Ben Daniels was the kind man who kept the tavern owner from cheating Gabriel and paid for him to spend the night at the tavern.

It was Ben who told him about Lexington and Concord.

It was Ben who told him to get off the road when travelers passed in order to avoid the soldiers.

It was Ben who said he knew something about Nathaniel that nobody else would know.

"Gabriel, did you have something you wanted to say?" asked Nathaniel, breaking the silence.

"I know Ben Daniels," said Gabriel quickly. "I met him at the King's Bridge Tavern right after I left New York. Ben is a farmer, and he owns land on the northern part of Manhattan Island." The words raced out of Gabriel's mouth in his desperate attempt to convince Washington and Greene he was telling the truth. "He told me to find you when I got to Boston," continued Gabriel.

"Well, that is interesting," said Nathaniel, scratching his chin. "Ben is my cousin, but I am not sure—"

"I KNOW ABOUT THE FISH!" exclaimed Gabriel, cutting Nathaniel Greene off mid-sentence.

"The fish?" questioned Nathaniel. "What in heaven's name are you talking about, boy?" The three men looked at each other in confused disbelief. "Well, I think that settles it," said Nathaniel. "This young lad has either swallowed too much of the river or is just simply out of his mind. We should be on our way, General. Come now, Gabriel, I think there's a homestead a few miles from here where we can drop you off. We might be able to spend the night there, considering how late it's getting."

"NO!" shouted Gabriel, as Nathaniel began to grab his arm to lead him to his horse. "I know about the codfish you said you caught out in the bay when you were a boy!" Nathaniel stopped tugging on his arm, and all three men stood silent.

"You went out on a rowboat with Ben," he continued desperately, "and you told everyone how you caught an enormous thirty-pound codfish with line and bait. It was all you could do to reel it into your boat, you said. But I know the truth: the crazy fish just jumped into your boat. Ben Daniels told me that story about you. He told me when I met him at the King's Bridge Tavern. He said you would want proof of who I was and the story about the codfish ought to do."

Nathaniel let go of Gabriel's arm. Gabriel knew his future was at the complete mercy of Nathaniel Greene. It would certainly be easy enough for him to pretend Gabriel's story was nothing but nonsense, especially since the commanding general of the Continental Army was standing right next to him. All he would have to say is that he didn't know what

Gabriel was talking about. The others would certainly believe him over Gabriel.

General Washington looked at Nathaniel and then at Gabriel. "Well," Washington said, "I guess that leaves nothing to doubt . . . a thirty-pound codfish just jumping into some-one's boat? I've never heard of such a crazy and outlandish tale. And to think I half-believed you'd walked all the way from New York. If it had been true, who knows, I might have asked you to stay. But . . . a thirty-pound codfish jumping into a boat? Well . . ." Washington's voice was trailing off to laughter. He turned now and grabbed Gabriel's arm to lead him off to the nearby horses. Gabriel tried to drag his feet, but it was no use.

They took several steps toward the horses when, all of the sudden, Gabriel heard Nathaniel say, "STOP!"

Washington and Artemas turned back around and looked at Nathaniel, who had not joined them in making their way to the horses. "It's true," said Nathaniel softly. "What Gabriel said is true. A huge codfish *did* jump into my boat when I was out fishing with my cousin Ben. I must have been about Gabriel's age when it happened. I went back and told everyone I caught it on my line. Ben knew the truth, but I asked him not to say anything. He didn't, at least not until he told our young master Gabriel at the King's Bridge Tavern on his way from New York to Boston." Nathaniel was now smiling at Gabriel. He reached out a hand and grabbed Gabriel's shoulder. He gave it a shake and then drew him near.

Washington and Artemas stood in stunned silence. "You mean a thirty-pound codfish just jumped into your boat?" asked Artemas, chuckling.

"Yes, a thirty-pound codfish did just jump into our boat," replied Nathaniel, emphatically.

"And you just told everyone you caught it?" Artemas asked again.

"YES!" responded Nathaniel. "It was a lie, and I know it. Ben and I didn't think anyone would believe the fish just jumped into our boat, so we figured one of us might as well get credit for it. It was the biggest codfish catch on line and bait in my hometown, at least so everyone thought."

"Well, Mr. Greene, that is quite a story," said Washington, chuckling now. "And to think I would have never heard of an enormous codfish jumping into a boat if it hadn't been for Gabriel here," Washington said, raising an eyebrow to Nathaniel. "Gabriel, I think we owe you an apology. I would certainly like to hear more about your journey from New York, but first, I would like us all to ride back to headquarters in Cambridge. Hop onto my horse. You'll have to sit behind me."

Gabriel was speechless. He simply sprang up onto Washington's stunning white horse and waited for the others to mount.

As he sat there, Thomas Tew's treasure returned to his mind. He could see shadowy outlines of the great trees lining the banks of the river. One of them might have held the treasure, but he had found something more precious than gold or silver. He had found Nathaniel Greene and General Washington, and soon, he'd be with the militia in Cambridge. It was strange how he'd been seeking one treasure but found another. His mother always told him the best treasures in life are the ones that find you. She was right.

As they rode away from the river, Gabriel put the thought of Thomas Tew's treasure out of his mind—a treasure that was meant to be found by someone else. He'd found his own treasure—or rather, the treasure had found him.

★19★

CAMP AT CAMBRIDGE

Gabriel could hardly believe he was riding on the back of the commanding general's horse. He could tell there was something different about the man, so tall he towered over Nathaniel Greene and Artemas Greenwood. Still, Gabriel didn't know what this man had done to earn the position of commanding general over all of the militias. He had also never heard the militia called the Continental Army before. He knew a Continental Congress had met to decide what the colonies should do about King George, but he was unsure how this Continental Army had been formed.

These questions rattled around inside his head as they rode through the night. The stars were shining brightly, and Washington, leading the way, seemed to know exactly where he was going. It amazed Gabriel how much faster they traveled by horse. What would have taken hours on foot took only a few minutes by horseback.

He heard the hoof beats of Washington's horse and those of Nathaniel's and Artemas's trailing behind. It had been a long time since Gabriel rode a horse. He'd learned to ride when he was very young. His father had to travel to buy books for his bookstore, and sometimes Gabriel accompanied him on trips to pick them up. He would ride the packhorse down to the docks where they would load books on its back, and then he'd ride home with his father, leading the packhorse along behind. He thought he was a good rider, but this was no packhorse, and General Washington rode swiftly, cutting his path through the trees. He knew he was riding with a master horseman.

After dodging through trees for most of their ride, the horses finally burst out onto a road. Ahead, lights glowed on the horizon. "Is that your camp, Your Excellency?" Gabriel asked.

"Yes," said Washington. "And you can just call me General, son. No need for the formality between you and me"

"Yes, sir—I mean . . . General." Gabriel was still a bit in awe of this grand officer.

As they approached Cambridge, Gabriel could now see some campfires glowing in the night. He looked into the houses, their windows lit by candlelight. As they rode closer now, he could see larger buildings and beautiful, stately mansions lying along a river shimmering under the starlight. All were fully lit and buzzing with activity. Gabriel asked, "What are those big buildings, General?"

"That is Harvard College," explained Washington. "Many of the troops are stationed in the buildings."

"Where are you staying, sir?" questioned Gabriel.

"In the house straight ahead," answered Washington.

Just ahead, a large house with several large windows, each glowing with candlelight, sat next to the river. Along the green and the banks of the river, campfires dotted the landscape. Their glowing embers reflected all manner of makeshift shelters. There were stick huts, lean-tos, and canvas tarps all scattered about the many campfires. Gabriel's heart cheered at the sight of this enormous army gathered in Cambridge, just waiting to fight.

As they rode by, smoke from the surrounding campfires lay heavy in the summer air, and the smell of roasting meat wafted up from the spits turning over the fires. Soldiers stared up from their campfires. Few, if any, had uniforms. Most men were dressed in common ditto suits, with tobacco brown jackets, waistcoats, and breeches, while others wore just their white shirts and trousers. Still others had deerskin jerkins and leggings. Some wore cowhide shoes or moccasins, but several were barefoot.

Men with gray hair, young boys, and all ages in between surrounded the fires. Most of the older men were clean-shaven, but many had tangled and matted hair. They sat cleaning their muskets and sharpening knives. One man played a fiddle while a woman danced around a fire. Men with bottles in hand cheered and sang along. A few of these soldiers stopped their frolicking as Washington rode by, giving hard, resentful looks. Gabriel wondered what these soldiers thought of this Virginian he was riding behind. But Washington did not seem to care what these men thought. He rode past quickly and quietly, making his way to the large house next to the river.

The horses galloped to the house, and two men immediately came out to grab and halter the horses. In stark contrast to the common soldiers they had just passed, these men were robed in brilliant white, frilled hunting shirts, cocked hats, and brown boots. One had a red cloth tied to his right shoulder. They saluted Washington as he dismounted.

"How was your ride, Your Excellency?" asked one of the men as he took off the saddle.

"It was an adventurous evening, to say the least, Sergeant," responded Washington. "Where did the boy come from, General?" asked the other man taking Nathaniel Greene's horse.

"New York," answered Nathaniel.

"New York?" said the man taking the horse, with complete disbelief.

"Yes, Sergeant, New York," said Washington. "Don't ask how he came from New York. You wouldn't believe the answer, anyway."

The horses were led away. Washington turned to his companions. "Gentlemen," he said, "we have had a full day, and I propose we turn in for the night. Artemas, I was wondering if you wouldn't mind accommodating our guest, Gabriel, tonight. Is there room in your tent? I know you have your son Jonathon with you, but I honestly don't know exactly what to do with the lad. We can talk more about it in the morning."

"Yes, sir," said Artemas. "Housing the young man who saved my life certainly won't be a problem. I'd say it's the least I can do."

"Very well, then," said Washington. "Can we all meet in my office here at the Vassall House at seven o'clock tomorrow morning? I would like to discuss young Mr. Cooper's future. Nathaniel, I want you and Artemas in the meeting, as well. Your thoughts on the matter are important to me."

Then men saluted the general. A bit delayed, Gabriel followed suit by flinging his hand up to his cap. Washington gave a hint of a smile directly to Gabriel, returned the salute, and turned. Gabriel was exhausted, and he knew the general must have also been tired. Yet, Washington's manner of walk seemed more youthful and athletic than that of a man of forty-two years. His long legs strode up the steps to the house. As he entered through the door, the sentries came to attention.

With that, Gabriel felt himself breathe again. He knew he had been in the presence of a great man. While filled with joy and amazement, Gabriel also felt a surge of sorrow, for he wanted to go run and tell his mother and father what just happened. He had just ridden with the commander in chief, the man who was in charge of driving the redcoats from Boston. They would have been proud, indeed.

Nathaniel and Artemas led him toward the tents across the street where several campfires were still aglow. Nathaniel stopped at a large tent close to Washington's house. "Good night, Gabriel," said Greene. "Get a good night's rest, lad. You've had quite a day, indeed." With that, Nathaniel Greene stepped into his tent.

Gabriel liked Nathaniel Greene. He knew the only reason he was here was because Nathaniel had plucked him from the river and then admitted—in front of George Washington—that he'd lied about catching the fish when he was a boy. Gabriel recognized how easy it would have been for Nathaniel to continue the lie about the fish, but he also recognized how much of Washington's respect he had earned by telling the truth.

Gabriel and Artemas walked on past several other campsites in Greene's regiment. Unlike the haphazard shelters they had seen earlier, Greene's men set their shelters in well-ordered, neat rows. There was a campfire in front of every three or four campsites. A white flag hung by one of the shelters. Its corner held a blue canton filled with yellow stars. The symbol of an anchor was sewn in the middle with the word "HOPE" written above.

A few men sat by their campfires. They were clean-shaven and wore the same white frilled hunting shirts and brown trousers as the sentries at Washington's headquarters. One soldier smiled at Artemas as he passed. "Got another young one there with you, Artemas? Where did you find this one?"

Artemas chuckled. "It's a long story. Ask me again in the morning after I've had a chance to let these weary bones rest."

"Fair enough," answered the soldier.

Gabriel whispered up to Artemas. "These men are dressed all the same. Are they all from the same militia?"

"They are all Rhode Islanders. Fine soldiers, every one of them. If you stick around here long enough, you're apt to see all manner of men, some good and some not so good."

Artemas led Gabriel to a tent of white canvas near the end of the row, with a fire glowing outside. There was a boy sitting by the fire. He was about Gabriel's height, with sandy brown hair and a spindly build. He was wearing a clean, white linen shirt and blue linen breeches and held a piece of meat over the flame with a stick.

The boy set the stick down on a rock next to the fire and jumped up. Artemas went over to him and gave him a hug. Artemas Greenwood looked nothing like the boy he embraced. Thick and stocky with dark hair and swarthy skin, he looked as rugged as an old grizzled badger, but his eyes glinted with joy.

"Sorry it took so long to get back, Jonathon, but my horse thought I needed to go for a swim," Artemas said.

"You look dry to me, Pa. I saved you some meat." Jonathon held up the stick to his father. Artemas tore the meat in two and gave half to Gabriel.

"Jonathon," said Artemas, "I would like you to meet Gabriel Cooper. Mr. Cooper has traveled from New York City all by himself to join us in the fight. And bless him, he saved me from being flung over a towering waterfall and dashed upon the rocks."

Jonathon gave his father a puzzled look and then turned to Gabriel. With a respectful nod of his head, he spoke. "Good to meet you, Gabriel Cooper."

"Good to meet you, as well." Gabriel nodded in return.

"You really saved my pa's life?" asked Jonathon.

"Well . . . I . . . I guess so," said Gabriel.

"There's no guessing about it, son," said Artemas. "Had it not been for the gallant Gabriel here, I would not be stand-ing before you getting ready to partake of this wonderful piece of meat you have saved for me." With that, Artemas dug his teeth into the meat and sat down by the fire. Gabriel did the same, savoring every bite, since he had not eaten since morning.

"Jonathon here plays the fife," said Artemas. "He wanted to come along with me when we left Rhode Island with General Greene. 'Course his mum had a fit about him com-ing along, but I promised to keep him safe and sound and said we'd be back home before the fall harvest."

"Do you really think the troops will leave Boston by this fall?" asked Gabriel.

"I most certainly do," said Artemas. "After the licking they took at Breed's Hill, King George will be callin' them back to the Motherland any day now."

Gabriel was astonished by Mr. Greenwood's statement. "Um, Mr. Greenwood," he said hesitantly, "I heard the patriots were driven from Breed's Hill. The ground was lost."

"Is that what you heard?" said Artemas. "Well if it is, you heard wrong. His Majesty's troops lost more soldiers and officers in that battle than they did over the past hundred years. We did lose the ground, that's true. But this war isn't about gaining ground. It's about ridding ourselves of these trespassing lobsterbacks!"

"Did you and Jonathon fight at Breed's Hill?" asked Gabriel.

"We did," said Artemas proudly. "Jonathon played his fife to keep the men's spirits up, as the regulars were marching up the hill with bayonets fixed. I was standing beside him, making sure no musket balls came his way. We stood through the first and second charges up to the ramparts. Then, for lack of lead, we had to fall back to Bunker Hill. After that, we retreated to our camp here, but not before we dealt His Majesty's finest plenty of death and destruction."

Gabriel looked at Jonathon now across the fire. He imagined himself on top of that hill, beating his drum just as

Jonathon had played his fife. It seemed so glorious to Gabriel but truly frightening at the same time. He wondered if Jonathon had been frightened and couldn't help but asking softly, "Were you scared?"

Jonathon shot a look at his father and then back at Gabriel. "Well, a little," he said, "but I knew my pa was right beside me, and he's one of the best shots in Rhode Island. Besides, I knew those soldiers had more important targets on their minds than a twelve-year-old with a fife."

"We are near the same in years," said Gabriel, smiling.

"You're twelve?" asked Jonathon, excited.

"Yes," said Gabriel.

"When is your birth date?"

"The thirtieth of July," responded Gabriel.

"As is my own!" said Jonathon.

"Well," said Artemas, "it looks like you two have a lot in common. I'd love stay up and hear it all, but I'm quite tuckered out from my swim in the river today. I think I'll turn in for the night. Gabriel, I would suggest you do the same soon. You don't want to be dragging your heels in the morning when you meet with General Washington."

"Yes, sir," responded Gabriel.

Artemas Greenwood entered the tent. Despite his father's advice, Jonathon kept Gabriel chatting by the fireside. Gabriel told Jonathon about his journey from New York. His new friend sat enraptured by his tale of adventure and told Gabriel more about camp life and the battle fought against the regulars on the hill over Boston.

The two carried on for hours until Gabriel's yawns finally grew so numerous he couldn't talk any longer. With firelight dimming, Gabriel and Jonathon stuck their heads inside the tent and laid down. Gabriel had not felt this kind of companionship since he left Malinda, Constance, and Mr. Fleming standing by their house in New Haven. He only hoped things could remain just as they were on this most wonderful night. He would have to wait until morning to find out.

★20★

THE DECISION

Morning light created a white glow through the canvas tent. Gabriel began to stir and saw he was the only one still in the tent. A horrible thought crossed his mind: had he somehow missed his meeting with General Washington? He quickly stuck his head outside to see Mr. Greenwood stoking the fire. Jonathon, walking toward the fire with a load of wood in his arms, saw him sticking his head out of the tent. "Good morning, Gabriel," he said.

"Morning," Gabriel said sleepily. His anxiety melted into relief seeing both Jonathon and Artemas still close-by.

The July air was already warm and muggy. The smoke from the fire seemed to hover just a few feet above the tops of their head, unable to escape the weight of the humid air. "We've got some beans to warm once we get the fire going," said Artemas. "It might do you good to go clean yourself up a bit in the Charles before we go to Vassall House this morning."

Artemas handed Gabriel a bar of lye soap and pointed toward the river. Gabriel had not washed with soap and water since his time at the Fleming farm. He took the soap from Mr. Greenwood and turned toward the river. "Don't dilly-dally, lad," shouted Artemas as he walked away. "You'll want to have a bite to eat before we report to the general."

Gabriel turned and nodded to Artemas and then went on his way. As he did, several men who were in earshot of Artemas's campsite gave him curious looks. He could guess what they were thinking: What would General Washington want with such a young boy, dirty and dressed in rags? He tried to ignore the stares and trudged off toward the river.

Up ahead he could see green sloping banks, and beyond, the murky water of the Charles River. Although the water's flow appeared gentle, Gabriel was not looking forward to stepping foot into a river once again. In the past few weeks, he had nearly drowned, not once, but twice. Still, he needed to clean himself, and the only way to accomplish this task was to get wet.

As he walked up to the river's edge, he saw other people near the water. Several women knelt along the bank, scrubbing laundry. They chattered away, paying no heed to Gabriel. Looking for a bit more privacy, he scanned the riverbank. He decided on an area of evergreen bushes clinging to the riverbank. Heading behind the bushes, he pulled off his torn and dirty clothes. The brush pricked at his skin as he walked into the water. As his feet hit the sandy bottom, he realized he was not the only one to pick this spot for a morning bath. Several militiamen were scattered about the river, and a pack of older boys had picked a spot upstream to hang a rope from a tree. They swung out over the water, dropping and splashing, one after another.

Feeling a sudden sense of urgency to get clean and get his clothes back on, Gabriel lathered up the soap. The lye in the soap burnt at every cut and scrape. Still, it made him feel fresh and clean, a feeling he had forgotten over the course of his journey. He rinsed off, hopped back into the bushes, and put his ragged clothes back on. Somehow, he didn't feel as clean once he was back in his old clothes. Still, he remembered Mr. Greenwood's words to hurry it up.

He scrambled back up to the rows of makeshift shelters. While all the militiamen looked so different, the lean-tos and huts all looked the same. He walked up several different rows until he finally saw the smoke hovering over a fire and recognized the Greenwoods' tent. Nathaniel Greene, in a clean new uniform, had joined Jonathon and Artemas at the fire.

Artemas turned and looked at him, handing him a tin cup full of beans. "Well, I'd like to say you look better boy, but I'm not one to fib."

"I scrubbed myself all over," responded Gabriel, handing the soap back to Mr. Greenwood.

"I believe you, but you still look like you just crawled out of a hole. Here, put this on," said Artemas. He gave Gabriel a fresh linen shirt. "This will have to do for now. I don't have a fresh pair of breeches. Let me look at your shoes."

Gabriel took the clean shirt from Mr. Greenwood and stuck out his feet. His shoes had holes in them in several different spots. "Those look well traveled, I'll say that," said Artemas. "Good shoes are a necessity to staying healthy. If General Washington doesn't send you back to New York, we will have to look into finding you a cordwainer. Do you have any coin left?" Gabriel looked down at his disheveled shoes and shook his head.

"No shillings, then?" said Artemas. "You made it all the way from New York to here with nary a farthing?"

"No, I had saved up, but, well . . . I, uh . . . lost it," responded Gabriel.

Jonathon turned to his father to explain. "Gabriel told me last night his coin pouch was swept away when he slept next to a river that flooded in the middle of the night."

"That's a story we have yet to hear," Nathaniel chimed in. "I still haven't figured out why you were standing next to the Charles River when Artemas was thrown from his horse. How did you end up so far off the road to Boston, anyway? That was a dense wood to be walking through."

Gabriel had been hoping no one would ask this question. He hadn't even told Jonathon about his search for Thomas Tew's treasure or how he'd thought he saw the ghost. He thought for a moment and then responded, "I was lost."

Nathaniel looked at him quizzically, "Lost . . . Well, how did you get lost?"

Gabriel still didn't want to tell Nathaniel or Artemas about how he'd left the road in search of Captain Tew's treasure. They might think he belonged in a hospital for the insane instead of the Continental Army. Still, he had to tell them something.

"I . . . uh . . . I just decided to follow the river when I heard it next to the road."

Nathaniel was growing impatient, "Gabriel, we can be here all morning if you continue to give me half-answers. Now, I would like to know the whole story as to why you were standing along that river when Artemas here came floating down."

"I wasn't exactly floating," said Artemas. "It was more like tumbling."

Nathaniel gave a smirk to Artemas and then said even more impatiently, "Floating, flailing, tumbling . . . whatever it was, why were you there?"

Gabriel knew there was no way to go on giving veiled answers, so he blurted out, "I was looking for Captain Thomas Tew's treasure. I didn't have any more coppers and was desperate. A man at a tavern in Marlborough told me he was Thomas Tew's grandson. He said Captain Tew hid part of his treasure along the Charles River after being chased down by bandits."

Gabriel waited for Nathaniel's reaction. There was a moment of sustained silence as Nathaniel Greene sat across the fire, straight-faced. Then there was a slow grin and a slight chuckle. After that, Nathaniel Greene burst out laughing. Artemas soon joined in.

"What's so funny?" asked Gabriel

"That crazy legend is as old as the hills." Nathaniel laughed. "I can just picture some old cantankerous devil of a man sitting in that tavern telling you the story of how those bandits chased after Thomas Tew and how he must have buried the treasure someplace before being shot by the bandits. Did he tell you Captain Tew had a peg leg and a parrot on his shoulder, too?" With this snide comment, Artemas and Nathaniel nearly rolled over laughing.

"What about the ghost? Did he tell you Captain Tew's ghost still prowls the river with his sword drawn, looking for the bandits?" chimed in Artemas, barely able to breathe from his laughter.

Gabriel sat watching in disgust. He was angry at their response. Thomas the Terrible was real, and the ghost of Thomas Tew seemed real to Gabriel at the time.

Finally beginning to catch his breath from laughter, Nathaniel said, "Gabriel, my lad, you've got to learn not to be so trusting of strangers. There is no such thing as Thomas Tew's treasure."

Gabriel couldn't hold his tongue. "How do you know?"

"I know because I grew up in Rhode Island. Captain Tew was a real Rhode Islander, all right, but he was a pirate and nothing more than that. He was a thief who stole valuable property from others. His son wasted whatever treasure was left on his own greedy lusts. Lies about what he did with his treasure have filled Rhode Island, and apparently all of New England, with wild stories, including the one you just told us."

Artemas contained his laughter and caught his breath. "Now, wait a minute, Nathaniel. If Gabriel hadn't followed that crazy pirate tale, he wouldn't have been at the river's edge, and I likely wouldn't be here today."

Despite Artemas's words, Gabriel still felt embarrassed and defensive. Much of what Thomas the Terrible had told him at the tavern was true. There had been a waterfall, a rocky cliff, and a trail around it, and there was an old oak tree with a hollow where a bag full of gold and silver might have been hidden, but none of that mattered now. What mattered were the words of Thomas the Terrible, and the search for Thomas Tew's treasure had led him here in a turn of events that he could never have even dreamed.

"I can understand why you were taken in," continued Nathaniel. "However, I would strongly suggest you not mention this search for treasure to General Washington, unless he specifically asks you. He's a Virginian and no doubt has never heard of the legend of Thomas Tew. He's liable not to find as much humor in it as do we." Nathaniel gave one last chuckle as he turned toward the Vassall House to see Washington. As Gabriel rose to follow, Jonathon patted him on his shoulder and gave an encouraging smile.

Gabriel, Artemas Greenwood, and Nathaniel Greene walked toward the large house by the river. Gabriel's stomach was churning. He said a silent prayer that things would go well. What would General Washington ask him? More importantly, what would he decide to do with him? What if he had found a new drum and drumsticks for him and asked him to play? He would run out of the room before he would beat on a drum in front of these men. What if the General told him he had to go back to New York? He would flatly refuse to do this, and he would find a way to stay.

A sentry stood at the top of the steps by the door to the house. Nathaniel greeted him as he climbed up the steps to the porch.

"General Greene," said the sentry, "good to see you, sir. General Washington is waiting for you in his office."

"Thank you," replied Greene, and the three entered through the front door of the house. There was a large entryway with stairs leading up to a second floor. To the right was an open doorway leading into what looked like a dining room. There was a large wooden table with a candle chandelier hanging over the top. On the other side of the table was a desk with parchment scattered over the top. A quill and inkwell stood in the corner of the desk. Behind the desk sat Washington reading a letter with a troubled look upon his face. His frown disappeared when he looked up and saw Nathaniel, Artemas, and Gabriel standing at the door.

"Gentlemen, come in, come in," he said happily. "I was catching up on my letters. I'm becoming frustrated with Congress's inability to provide food and ammunition for this army. That should not concern any of you this fine morning, though. Sit down."

Three chairs sat in front of Washington's desk. Nathaniel pulled out the middle chair for Gabriel, while he and Artemas sat on either side.

"Now then," began Washington, "what to do with Mr. Cooper here? I had hoped to say I'd given the matter much serious thought over the past twelve hours, but I must admit my failure to do so. Gabriel, you wish to remain here in Cambridge as a part of this army, is that true?"

"Very much so, sir," responded Gabriel.

"Gabriel," continued Washington, "we have a battle ahead of us that will kill and wound good men. Men will die, and if you join this army, there's a chance you could die in its service. Do you understand this?"

"Yes, sir, I know, but I am here to do my part for the cause of liberty," said Gabriel.

"Do you know how to shoot a gun?" asked Washington.

"Well, sir, I've never actually shot one before, but I can learn. I read a book about different kinds of guns and cannon once from my father's bookstore."

"I see," said Washington. "And what do you know about military tactics, young Master Gabriel?"

"Well, sir, I do not know exactly what you mean, but I read a book once about the Battle of Marathon, where the Greeks surrounded and defeated the attacking Persians by using a special military maneuver."

"Ah, yes, the Greeks and the Persians. Then do you know how to wield a sword?" continued Washington.

"No, sir, I've never used a sword, but I also read a book about Japanese knights, called samurai. They carry very large swords to fight off their enemies."

"And what about military drill, do you know how to march?" asked Washington.

"No, sir, but—"

"Let me guess," said Washington, cutting him off. "You have never actually marched with a group of soldiers, but you read a book about that, too. Is that it?"

"Yes, sir," said Gabriel, his voice trailing off. His heart was sinking. General Washington had quickly realized he had done nothing to warrant him becoming a soldier.

"A horse? Do you know how to ride?" asked Washington.

"Yes, sir, I do know how to do that, and I haven't read any books about it, either," responded Gabriel eagerly.

"Gabriel, I must be honest with you. You do not fit the description of a soldier capable of lending support to this army," stated Washington. "What made you want to leave New York and walk to Boston in the first place?"

Gabriel swallowed hard and tried to think of a way to explain what had compelled him to go so far. Finally, he said, "There was not just one thing, sir. It had been building up inside of me. It's a feeling that is hard to explain, but it has to do with the unfairness of how the king and his men treated my family. Soldiers moved into my father's bookstore when the king said the colonists had to make their businesses available to his troops. I was much younger then, but I'll never forget the way they strutted around, proud as peacocks, all the while stealing our food. They said it was the king's justice, but all I saw was injustice. They treated us like the dirt beneath their feet. It's the same with the people loyal to the king. They think they are better than everyone else and that the king has been appointed by God as the heir to the throne of England and can do no wrong. That doesn't make any sense. The king is a man, same as you and I, and he has done wrong.

"When my parents died, a Reverend Loring brought me in to stay in his house. At dinner one evening, the reverend was going on about how King George was a good and noble leader and deserving of a toast honoring his benevolence. I refused, and called the king a tyrant. Mrs. Loring fainted, and the reverend was so mad he told me to leave his house at once.

I left that night. Reverend Loring probably would have taken me back in with a whipping and extra chores, I reckon, but I didn't want to go back. I thought of my mother and father. I thought of what my father would have done, and he would have fought for our freedom. I know, General, this is what my father would have done. And it is what I *must* do."

Washington sat at his desk in silence and then smiled, "Did Mrs. Loring really faint when you called the king a tyrant?"

"Yes, sir. She fell right out of her chair," responded Gabriel, smiling.

"Gabriel, I have no doubt your motives are pure and you have the heart of a true patriot," Washington said, rising from his chair at his desk. "But it takes more than just heart to be an asset to this army."

"Ahem, Your Excellency? If I may, sir," Artemas began, clearing his throat, "please do not forget the courage and clearness of mind under pressure that this young man displayed in saving my life."

"Oh, believe me, Artemas, I have not forgotten. Why do you think I am taking precious time to decide what should be done with young Master Cooper?"

Gabriel was trying to hold back his restlessness and remain still in his chair when someone knocked at the door to the room. A tall, thin man peered in through the crack in the door. "Sorry to bother you, sir, but you have previously asked

I bring correspondence from our French contacts directly and immediately to your attention. I have a letter here from a . . ." The man looked down awkwardly at the paper, staring at it, trying to decipher the name. " . . . a Monsieur Beaumar . . . Chais."

"Yes, Joseph, please bring it here. Excuse me a moment," said Washington to Artemas, Gabriel, and Nathaniel. The man marched in quickly, handed the letter to Washington, did an about-face, and was about to leave the room when Washington said, "Joseph, please don't leave us so quickly. Gabriel, let me introduce you. This is Joseph Reed. He is one of my few aides-de-camp here at Cambridge. He is a part of what I call my military family, as he resides here at headquarters and plays a central role in all we are trying to accomplish, namely driving the British from Boston. His duties encompass trying to help me with this intolerable task of letter writing, with which he is doing a fine job."

"Thank you, sir," responded Reed.

Gabriel felt a twinge of envy well up inside him. To live and work in this wonderful house that served as the headquarters for freedom, thinking of ways to defeat the king, his parents would be so proud.

"Mr. Reed," continued Washington, "seated on the right is Captain Artemas Greenwood, on the left is General Nathaniel Greene, whom I believe you know, and in the middle is our new young friend, Master Gabriel Cooper of New York. Now, before you scurry off, let me have a quick look at this letter." Washington glanced down at the letter, his eyes darting quickly all over the page. "Mr. Reed, I'm afraid I can understand but very little of this letter, as it is written in French. Why hasn't this been translated?"

"Sir," responded Reed, "it came directly to Cambridge instead of Philadelphia. With all these men here, we surely will find someone who can read French."

"Well, this won't do. As you know, Joseph, we are trying to establish contacts in France. Monsieur Beaumarchais is one of those contacts. I must know what this says," Washington said, clearly frustrated. "I don't know how Congress expects us to develop an alliance with France when we can't even read their letters!"

"May I see it, sir?" asked Gabriel, interrupting Washington's frustrated rant.

"Son, this is not one of your books!" responded Washington, hastily slapping the letter down on his desk.

"General, I would suggest you let him see it, sir," said Nathaniel.

Washington let out a sigh, slid the letter over to Gabriel, and then sat down behind his desk, slumping in his chair. Gabriel picked the letter up off Washington's desk, looked it over, and began to read it aloud.

""To the commanding chief of the Provincial military at Cambridge, I am Pierre-Augustin Caron de Beaumarchais. I am a businessman who is very happy' . . . no, I mean, 'interested in your fight for freedom.'"

"Sorry, sir, my French is not perfect," said Gabriel, looking up from the paper.

He continued reading again from the letter. "'I have been in prison at the hands of corrupt leaders. I am released, but stripped of my civil rights. Although my estate has been taken from me, I know of others here who have the desire, and the resources , to see you succeed in your pursuit of liberty. Should it please the commander who reads this, I wish to establish correspondence. I cannot offer this correspondence on behalf of Our Most Royal Majesty, Louis the XVI. I do have every confidence His Majesty will restore my civil rights, at which time I am sure my associations will look to your favor most kindly. Amicably, Monsieur Beaumarchais.'"

Gabriel put the letter carefully back on Washington's desk. Silence filled the room. Finally, Washington spoke. "Gabriel, I can't see the nose in front of my face. You told me your mother was from France when we first met, did you not?"

"Yes, sir," said Gabriel. "She taught me to read and write French. I can speak a little, but I haven't had much practice lately."

"Mr. Reed," said Washington, "that will do for now. I will draft a response to this letter after I have finished with Master Cooper here."

"Yes, sir," said Joseph Reed, leaving the room and shutting the door behind him.

"Gabriel, where did your mother come from in France?" asked Washington.

"I don't know, sir. She told me very little about her past. Only that she met my father when her parents took her on a trip to England. She was nineteen and decided not to return to France with her parents. That is all I know except what she told me about the ring and what she put in her last note to me."

"What ring?" asked Washington.

Gabriel hesitated for a moment. No one had ever asked to see his ring before. He always kept it tucked away so no one would know what he was carrying around in his pocket. Despite his hesitation, he knew he could trust Nathaniel, Artemas, and General Washington. He slowly reached into his pocket, pulled out the ring, and handed it to Washington.

Washington looked at it carefully, holding it up to his eyes and turning it over in his fingers. "What did your mother tell you about this ring?"

"That it is a family heirloom, sir. I think she said the stone was a sapphire."

"Is that all?" questioned Washington.

"Yes, sir," answered Gabriel.

"And the note, does it give any explanation about this ring?"

"No, sir," said Gabriel. "I just keep the note because my mother wrote it to me shortly before she died. I have never really figured out what she was trying to say, other than she loved me."

"I can see why she loved you, Gabriel," said Washington. "And I would never want to intrude into such a private note, but are you sure this note doesn't provide any further explanation of this ring?"

"Yes, sir, I'm sure," said Gabriel. "It doesn't say anything about a ring."

Washington sat silently, studying the ring for a moment longer. Then he carefully handed it back to Gabriel. "It is quite beautiful. I would hate for such a valuable item to become lost or, worse yet, stolen. Gabriel, keep your ring safe. It may be of great use to you someday."

Washington rose from his chair. "Very well, I guess that concludes our business here this morning, then," said Washington. "So much to do and so little time."

Nathaniel, Artemas, and Gabriel looked at one another curiously. The other two began to rise from their chairs slowly, but Gabriel did not budge.

"Sir, what do you mean?" asked Gabriel in a confused and panicked voice. "What's to become of me?"

Washington gave him a puzzled look. "What do you mean, what's to become of you? Isn't my decision good enough for you?"

"Excuse me, sir," said Nathaniel, "but I don't think you ever actually stated what your decision was."

"It must have been so obvious to me I forgot to say it aloud," chuckled Washington. "Is it not obvious to you?"

"No, sir," stated Gabriel plainly.

"Well, let me make it clear and official, then," said Washington with a ringing tone. "Master Gabriel Cooper, I would like to extend a formal invitation for you to be one of my aides. As part of this job, you shall assist me in reading and writing the French language, and you shall assist me in whatever other military matters I may require. Understand this job may also present certain risks, and you may be asked to accomplish other tasks outside the confines of my head-quarters. You shall lodge here at this house, as I may need your assistance at any hour of the day. Do you understand the terms of this offer and accept this position?"

Gabriel sat in stunned silence for a moment, unsure whether he should laugh or cry from the joy welling up inside him. Finally, he jumped up from his chair. "I do—I mean, I will—I mean, YES, SIR!"

"You do not know how much it pleases me to hear you say that," said Washington with a smile across his face. "General Greene and Captain Greenwood, I expect you to be the guardians of Gabriel Cooper, as well. He shall be your charge as well as mine. Now Gabriel, why don't you take a break from the stuffy air of this room and go tell Mr. Greenwood's son you are an official member of this army and, more importantly, part of my personal staff. Report back here promptly at three o' clock, and let's draft a response to our new friend Monsieur Beaumarchais. After that, you shall eat dinner here so I can introduce you to some other officers you will need to know. Can I expect you at three, then?"

"Yes, sir," said Gabriel, barely holding back his excitement. He had never imagined a more glorious ending to his journey. A smile beamed across his face.

"Good, then," said Washington. "I will see you soon, Gabriel, and I am looking forward to our adventures together."

Gabriel turned and was ready to run out of the room and scream with excitement, when Washington gave a shout.

"Wait, Gabriel. There is one more thing. I about forgot to give this back to you. It's your drum, or what's left of it."

Washington handed the mangled drum to Gabriel. Gabriel took it from Washington and held it lightly in his hands. As he looked at it, his entire journey played back through his mind. It was this drum that brought him here—a place filled with excitement, adventure, and people who would become his new family. Overcome with emotion, Gabriel's eyes welled up with tears.

"I am so sorry," said Washington. "If I had seen it sooner along the path, I might have been able to steer my horse around it. Take heart, though. I'd much rather have you as an aide than a drummer boy."

Gabriel looked up, "These are tears of joy, not sadness. Without this drum, I'd not be standing here. It has brought me a long way."

"Yes, it certainly has done that," responded Washington.

Gabriel wiped his eyes, saluted, and then turned to run out the door with the broken drum in hand. He didn't shout or scream with excitement, though, and he didn't run to tell Jonathon the news, either. Instead, Gabriel went alone to the riverbank. There, he took one last look at the drum and then tossed it into the water. It floated along for a while before sinking out of view. He stood silently and watched it disappear. In a way, it was as if he was saying goodbye to a good friend, but he wasn't sad. The drum had served its purpose, and now he was just returning it.

Watching the drum fade away reminded Gabriel that, for every end, there is a beginning. He knew his beginning was bright.

While Gabriel Cooper is a fictional character, there really were boys like Gabriel who joined in the fight against England. Most came with their fathers or brothers, while a few, like Gabriel, came by themselves. Jonathon Greenwood was one of those real boys who made his way by himself from Portland, Maine, to Boston as a fifer. Jonathon's father, Artemas Greenwood, is, therefore, a fictional character but represents how most boys came to be part of the army surrounding Boston. The majority of these boys were fifers or drummers who proudly played while the men around them marched into battle. The historical characters along Gabriel's journey, such as Benedict Arnold, Nathaniel Greene, and George Washington, are given their true place in the timeline of the Revolution. The battles that Gabriel hears about along his journey are also set in the proper place and time. And there really was a man named Thomas Tew who was a Rhode Island privateer turned pirate. As for his ghost, I will leave it up to you to decide whether that is real or not.

GLOSSARY

bayonette (BAY-uh-net)—a long knife that can be fastened to the end of a rifle

epaulettes (EP-uh-lettes)—ornamental shoulder pieces worn on uniforms, chiefly by military officers

lobsterbacks (LOB-ster-baks)—British soldiers; *lobsterback* refers to the red color of cooked lobsters and the red jacket of the British uniform

loyalists (LOI-uh-lists)—colonists who were loyal to Great Britain during the Revolutionary War

militia (muh-LISH-uh)—a group of citizens who are trained to fight but who serve in a time of emergency

musket (MUHSS-kit)—a gun with a long barrel that was used before the rifle was invented

Parliament (PAR-luh-muhnt)—the group of British officials that makes laws for Great Britain

patriot (PAY-tree-uht)—an American colonist who wanted independence from Britain

quinine (KWYE-nine)—a white, bitter, crystal-like substance used as medicine

redcoats (RED-kohts)—British soldiers, named after the color of their uniforms

skirmish (SKUR-mish)—a minor fight in a battle

Tory (TOHR-ee)—a person who supported the British cause in the Revolutionary War

treason (TREE-zuhn)—the crime of betraying your country

whortleberries (WHOR-tuhl-BER-ees)—small edible berries that are sweet and blackish in color

DISCUSSION QUESTIONS

1. What was Gabriel's destiny? Explain how the discarded drum brought Gabriel to his destiny.

2. What is the theme, or central idea, of Gabriel's story? Explain your answer.

3. The author used third-person point of view to tell Gabriel's story. How would the story be different if he had chosen to use first-person?

WRITING PROMPTS

1. Pretend you are Gabriel and write a one- to two-page letter to Herbert Loring outlining everything that has happened since you left the Loring home.

2. When was Gabriel most at risk? Write an essay explaining your answer, using details from the novel.

3. The author was inspired by the real heroes and villains of the Revolutionary War. Research a person from this era, and write either a short biography or historical fictional story about him or her. Use at least three different sources in your research.

CHRIS STEVENSON

Chris Stevenson is not only an author, but also an attorney, a pilot, and a farmer. He lives on a farm in Tippecanoe County, Indiana, with his wife and five sons. Chris developed a newfound love of history when he began to listen to books about the American Revolution on his commute to his law firm. He realized how many wonderful stories could be told about real events and people and how, as a kid, he had missed out on what history was really all about. Wanting his boys to hear and learn about some of the amazing people and events of the Revolution, Chris began telling his sons bedtime stories about a boy named Gabriel Cooper. When they kept wanting more Gabriel stories, Chris decided to start writing his first historical fiction novel, *The Drum of Destiny*.